THE CASE OF THE LATE PIG

THE CASE OF THE LATE PIG

Margery Allingham

All the characters and events portrayed in this work are fictitious.

THE CASE OF THE LATE PIG

A Felony & Mayhem mystery

PRINTING HISTORY
First UK edition (Hodder & Stoughton): 1937
First U.S. edition (Penguin): 1940
Felony & Mayhem edition: 2008

ISBN: 978-1-934609-14-9

Manufactured in the United States of America

For
Mr. Malcolm Johnson
from
Mr. Albert Campion

The icon above says you're holding a copy of a book in the Felony & Mayhem "Vintage" category. These books were originally published prior to about 1965, and feature the kind of twisty, ingenious puzzles beloved by fans of Agatha Christie and John Dickson Carr. If you enjoy this book, you may well like other "Vintage" titles from Felony & Mayhem Press, including:

MARGERY ALLINGHAM
The Crime at Black Dudley
Mystery Mile
Look to the Lady
Police at the Funeral
Sweet Danger
Death of a Ghost
Flowers for the Judge
Dancers in Mourning

EDMUND CRISPIN
The Case of the Gilded Fly
Holy Disorders
Swan Song
Love Lies Bleeding

ELIZABETH DALY
Murders in Volume 2
Evidence of Things Seen
Nothing Can Rescue Me

MATTHEW HEAD
The Devil in the Bush
The Cabinda Affair

For more about these books, and other Felony & Mayhem titles, or to place an order, please visit our website at

www.FelonyAndMayhem.com

or contact us at

Felony and Mayhem Press
156 Waverly Place
New York, NY 10014

Contents

THE CASE OF THE LATE PIG

CHAPTER 1

The Invitations to the Funeral Were Informal

THE MAIN THING TO REMEMBER in autobiography, I have always thought, is not to let any damned modesty creep in to spoil the story. This adventure is mine, Albert Campion's, and I am fairly certain that I was pretty nearly brilliant in it in spite of the fact that I so nearly got myself and old Lugg killed that I hear a harp quintet whenever I consider it.

It begins with me eating in bed.

Lord Powne's valet took lessons in elocution and since then has read *The Times* to His Lordship while His Lordship eats his unattractive nut-and-milk breakfast.

Lugg, who in spite of magnificent qualities has elements of the Oaf about him, met His Lordship's valet in the Mayfair mews pub where they cater for gentlemen in the service of gentlemen and was instantly inspired to imitation. Lugg has not taken lessons in elocution, at least not since he left Borstal in the reign of Edward the Seventh. When he came into my service he was a parole man with a stupendous record of misplaced bravery and ingenuity. Now he reads *The Times* to me when I eat, whether I like it or not.

Since his taste does not run towards the literary in journalism he reads to me the only columns in that paper which do appeal to him. He reads the Deaths.

"Peters…" he read, heaving his shirt-sleeved bulk between me and the light. "Know anyone called Peters, cock?"

I was reading a letter which had interested me particularly because it was both flowery and unsigned and did not hear him, so presently he laid down the paper with gentle exasperation.

"Answer me, can't you?" he said plaintively. "What's the good of me trying to give this place a bit of tone if you don't back me up? Mr. Turke says 'Is Lordship is most attentive during the readings. He chews everything 'e eats forty times before 'e swallers and keeps 'is mind on everything that's being read to 'im."

"So I should think," I said absently. I was taken by the letter. It was not the ordinary anonymous filth by any means.

> *"Peters—R. I. Peters, aged 37, on Thursday the 9th, at Tethering, after a short illness. Funeral, Tethering Church, 2:30 Saturday. No flowers. Friends will accept this as the only intimation."*

Lugg reads horribly and with effect.
The name attracted me.

"Peters?" I said, looking up from the letter with interest. "R. I. Peters…Pig Peters. Is it in there?"

"Oh, my *gawd!*" Lugg threw down the paper in disgust. "You're a philistine, that's what you are, a ruddy phylis. After a perishing short illness, I keep tellin' you. Know 'im?"

"No," I said cautiously. "Not exactly. Not now."

Lugg's great white moon of a face took on an ignoble expression.

"I get you, Bert," he said smugly, tucking his chins into his collarless neck. "Not quite our class."

Although I realize that he is not to be altered, there are things I dare not pass.

"Not at all," I said with dignity. "And don't call me 'Bert.'"

"All right." He was magnanimous. "Since you've asked me, cock, I won't. Mr. Albert Campion to the world: Mr. Albert to me. What about this bloke Peters we was discussin'?"

"We were boys together," I said. "Sweet, downy, blue-eyed little fellows at Botolph's Abbey. Pig Peters took three square inches of skin off my chest with a rusty penknife to show I was his branded slave. He made me weep till I was sick and I kicked him in the belly, whereupon he held me over an unlighted gas jet until I passed out."

Lugg was shocked.

"There was no doings like that at our college," he said virtuously.

"That's the evil of State control," I said gently, not anxious to appear unkind. "I haven't seen Peters since the day I went into the sicker with CO poisoning, but I promised him then I'd go to his funeral."

He was interested at once.

"I'll get out your black suit," he said obligingly. "I like a funeral—when it's someone you know."

I was not really listening to him. I had returned to the letter.

*Why should he die? He was so young. There
are thousands more fitting than he for the journey.
"Peters, Peters," saith the angel. "Peters, Pietro,
Piero, come," saith the angel. Why? Why should
he follow him? He that was so strong, so unpre-
pared, why should he die? The roots are red in
the earth and the century creepeth on its way.
Why should the mole move backwards?—it is not
yet eleven.*

It was typewritten on ordinary thin quarto, as are all these
things, but it was not ill-spelt and the punctuation was meticulous, which was an unusual feature in my experience. I showed
it to Lugg.

He read it through laboriously and delivered himself of his
judgement with engaging finality.

"Bit of the Prayer Book," he said. "I remember learning it
when I was a nipper."

"Don't be an ass," I said mildly, but he coloured and his
little black eyes sank into my head.

"Call me a liar," he said truculently. "Go on, call me a liar
and then I'll do a bit of talking."

I know him in these moods and I realized from experience
that it was impossible to shake him in a theory of this sort.

"All right," I said. "What does it mean?"

"Nothing," he said with equal conviction.

I tried another tack.

"What's the machine?"

He was helpful at once.

"A *Royal* portable, new or newish, no peculiarities to
speak of. Even the E is as fresh as that bit of 'addock you've left.

Paper's the ordinary Plantag. They sell reams of it everywhere. Let's see the envelope. London Wc1," he continued after a pause. "That's the old central stamp. Clear, isn't it? The address is from the telephone book. Chuck it in the fire."

I still held the letter. Taken in conjunction with the announcement in *The Times* it had, it seemed to me, definite points of interest. Lugg sniffed at me.

"Blokes like you who are always getting theirselves talked about are bound to get anonymous letters," he observed, allowing the critical note in his tone to become apparent. "While you remained strictly amateur you was fairly private, but now you keep runnin' round with the busies, sticking your nose into every bit of blood there is about, and you're gettin' talked of. We'll 'ave women sittin' on the stairs waitin' for you to sign their names on piller-cases so they can embroider it if you go on the way you are going. Why can't you take a quiet couple o' rooms in a good neighbour'ood and play poker while you wait for your titled relative to die? That's what a gentleman would do."

"If you were female and could cook I'd marry you," I said vulgarly. "You nag like a stage wife."

That silenced him. He got up and waddled out of the room, the embodiment of dignified disgust.

I read the letter through again after I had eaten and it sounded just as light-headed. Then I read *The Times* announcement.

R. I. Peters... It was Pig all right. The age fitted in. I remembered him booting us to persuade us to call him "Rip." I thought of us as we were then, Guffy Randall and I and Lofty and two or three others. I was a neat little squirt with sleek white hair and goggles; Guffy was a tough for his age, which was ten and a quarter; and Lofty, who is now holding down his seat in the Peers with a passionate determination more creditable than necessary, was a cross between a small tapir and a more ordinary porker.

Pig Peters was a major evil in our lives at that time. He ranked with Injustice, The Devil, and Latin Prose. When Pig Peters fed the junior study fire with my collection of skeleton leaves I earnestly wished him dead, and, remembering the incident that morning at breakfast, I was mildly surprised to find that I still did.

Apparently he was, too, according to *The Times*, and the discovery cheered me up. At twelve he was obese, red, and disgusting, with sandy lashes, and at thirty-seven I had no doubt he had been the same.

Meanwhile there was the sound of heavy breathing in the outer room and Lugg put his head round the door.

"Cock," he said in a tone of diffident friendliness which showed that all was forgiven, "I've had a squint at the map. See where Tethering is? Two miles west of Kepesake. Going down?"

I suppose it was that which decided me. At Highwaters, in the parish of Kepesake, there lives Colonel Sir Leo Pursuivant, Chief Constable of the county and an extremely nice old boy. He has a daughter, Janet Pursuivant, whom I like still in spite of everything.

"All right," I said. "We'll drop in at Highwaters on our way back."

Lugg was in complete agreement. They had a nice piece of home-cured last time he was there, he said.

We went down in state. Lugg wore his flattest bowler, which makes him look like a thug disguised as a plain-clothes man, and I was remarkably neat myself.

Tethering was hardly *en fête*. If you consider three square miles of osier swamp surrounding a ploughed hill on which five cottages, a largish house, and an ancient church crowd on each other's toes in order to keep out of a river's uncertain bed you have Tethering pretty accurately in your mind.

The churchyard is overgrown and pathetic and when we saw it in late winter it was a sodden mass of dead cow-parsley. It was difficult not to feel sorry for Pig. He always had grand ideas, I remember, but there was nothing of pomp in his obsequies.

We arrived late—it is eighty miles from Town—and I felt a trifle loutish as I pushed open the mouldering lich-gate and, followed by Lugg, stumbled over the ragged grass towards the little group by the grave.

The parson was old and I suspected that he had come on the bicycle I had seen outside the gate, for the skirts of his cassock were muddy.

The sexton was in corduroys and the bearers in dungarees.

The other members of the group I did not notice until afterwards. A funeral is an impressive business even among the marble angels and broken columns of civilization. Here, out of the world in the rain-soaked silence of a forgotten hillside, it was both grim and sad.

As we stood there in the light shower the letter I had received that morning faded out of my mind. Peters had been an ordinary unlovable sort of twirp, I supposed, and he was being buried in an ordinary unloved way. There was really nothing curious about it.

As the parson breathed the last words of the service, however, an odd thing happened. It startled me so much that I stepped back on Lugg and almost upset him.

Even at twelve and a half Pig had had several revolting personal habits and one of them was a particularly vicious way of clearing his throat. It was a sort of hoarse rasping noise in the larynx, followed by a subdued whoop and a puff. I cannot describe it any more clearly but it was a distinctive sort of row and one I never heard made by anyone else. I had completely forgotten it, but just as we were turning away from the yawning grave into which the coffin had been lowered I heard it distinctly after what must have been twenty years. It brought Pig back to my mind with a vividness which was unnerving and I gaped round at the rest of us with my scalp rising.

Apart from the bearers, the parson, the sexton, Lugg, and myself there were only four other people present and they all looked completely innocent.

There was a pleasant solid-looking person on my left and a girl in rather flashy black beyond him. She was more sulky than tearful and appeared to be alone. She caught my eye and smiled at me as I glanced at her and I looked on past her at the old man in the topper who stood in a conventional attitude of grief which was rather horrible because it was so unconvincing. I don't know when I took such a dislike to a fellow. He had little grey curly moustaches which glittered in the rain.

My attention was distracted from him almost at once by the discovery that the fourth unaccountable was Gilbert Whippet. He had been standing at my elbow for ten minutes and I had not seen him, which was typical of him.

Whippet was my junior at Botolph's Abbey and he followed me to the same school. I had not seen him for twelve or fourteen years, but, save that he had grown, of course, he was unchanged.

It is about as easy to describe Whippet as it is to describe water or a sound in the night. Vagueness is not so much his characteristic as his entity. I don't know what he looks like, except that presumably he has a face, since it would be an omission that I should have been certain to observe. He had on some sort of grey-brown coat which merged with the dead cow-parsley and he looked at me with that vacancy which is yet recognition.

"Whippet!" I said. "What are you doing here?"

He did not answer and unconsciously I raised my hand to clip him. He never did answer until he was clipped and the force of habit was too much for me. Fortunately I restrained myself in time, recollecting that the years which had elapsed between our meeting had presumably given him ordinary rights of citizenship. All the same I felt unreasonably angry with him and I spoke sharply.

"Whippet, why did you come to Pig's funeral?" I said.

He blinked at me and I was aware of round pale grey eyes.

"I—er—I was invited, I think," he said in the husky diffident voice I remembered so well and which conveyed that he was not at all sure what he was talking about. "I—I—had one this—this morning, don't you know..."

He fumbled in his coat and produced a sheet of paper. Before I read it I knew what it was. Its fellow was in my pocket.

"Odd," said Whippet, "about the mole, you know. Informal invitation. I—er—I came."

His voice trailed away, as I knew it would, and he wandered off, not rudely but carelessly, as though there was nothing to keep him in place. He left the note in my hand by mistake, I was convinced.

I came out of the churchyard at the end of the straggling procession. As we emerged into the lane the stolid, pleasant-looking person I had noticed glanced at me with enquiry in his eyes and I went over to him. The question in my mind was not an easy one and I was feeling around for some fairly inoffensive way of putting it when he helped me out.

"A sad business," he said. "Quite young. Did you know him well?"

"I don't know," I said, looking like an idiot, while he stared at me, his eyes twinkling.

He was a big chap, just over forty, with a square capable face.

"I mean," I said, "I was at school with an R. I. Peters and when I saw *The Times* this morning I realized I was coming down this way and I thought I might look in, don't you know."

He remained smiling kindly at me as if he thought I was mental and I floundered on.

"When I got here I felt I couldn't have come to the right—I mean I felt it must be some other Peters," I said.

"He was a big heavy man," he observed thoughtfully. "Deep-set eyes, too fat, light lashes, thirty-seven years old, went to a prep school at Sheepsgate and then on to Totham."

I was shocked. "Yes," I said. "That's the man I knew."

He nodded gloomily. "A sad business," he repeated. "He came to me after an appendix operation. Shouldn't have had it: heart wouldn't stand it. Picked up a touch of pneumonia on the way down and—" he shrugged his shoulders, "—couldn't save him, poor chap. None of his people here."

I was silent. There was very little to say.

"That's my place," he remarked suddenly, nodding towards the one big house. "I take a few convalescents. Never had a death there before. I'm in practice here."

I could sympathize with him and I did. It was on the tip of my tongue to ask him if Peters had let him in for a spot of cash.

He had not hinted it but I guessed there was some such matter in his thoughts. However, I refrained; there seemed no point in it.

We stood there chatting aimlessly for some moments, as one does on these occasions, and then I went back to Town. I did not call in at Highwaters after all, much to Lugg's disgust. It was not that I did not want to see Leo or Janet, but I was inexplicably rattled by Pig's funeral and by the discovery that it actually was Pig's. It had been a melancholy little ceremony which had left a sort of "half heard" echo in my ears.

The two letters were identical. I compared them when I got in. I supposed Whippet had seen *The Times* as I had. Still it was queer he should have put two and two together. And there had been that extraordinary cough and the revolting old fellow in the topper, not to mention the sly-eyed girl.

The worst thing about it was that the incident had recalled Pig to my mind. I turned up some old football groups and had a good look at him. He had a distinctive face. One could see even then what he was going to turn into.

I tried to put him out of my head. After all, I had nothing to get excited about. He was dead. I shouldn't see him again.

All this happened in January. By June I had forgotten the fellow. I had just come in from a session with Stanislaus Oates at the Yard, where we had been congratulating each other over the evidence in the Kingford shooting business which had just flowered into a choice bloom for the Judge's bouquet, when Janet rang up.

I had never known her hysterical before and it surprised me a little to hear her twittering away on the phone like a nest of sparrows.

"It's too filthy," she said. "Leo says you're to come at once. No, my dear—I can't say it over the phone, but Leo is afraid it's—Listen, Albert, it's M for mother, U for unicorn, R for rabbit, D for darling, E for—for egg, R for—"

"All right," I said, "I'll come."

Leo was standing on the steps of Highwaters when Lugg and I drove up. The great white pillars of the house, which was built by an architect who had seen the B.M. and never forgotten it, rose up behind him. He looked magnificent in his ancient shootin' suit and green tweed flowerpot hat—a fine specimen for anybody's album.

He came steadily down the steps and grasped my hand.

"My dear boy," he said, "not a word...not a word." He climbed in beside me and waved a hand towards the village. "Police station," he said. "First thing."

I've known Leo for some years and I know that the single-ness of purpose which is the chief characteristic in a delightful personality is not to be diverted by anything less than a covey of Mad Mullahs. Leo had one thing in his mind and one thing only. He had been planning his campaign ever since he had heard that I was on my way, and, since I was part of that campaign, my only hope was to comply.

He would not open his mouth save to utter road directions until we stood together on the threshold of the shed behind the police station. First he dismissed the excited bobbies in charge and then paused and took me firmly by the lapel.

"Now, my boy," he said, "I want your opinion because I trust you. I haven't put a thought in your mind, I haven't told you a particle of the circumstances, I haven't influenced you in any way, have I?"

"No, sir," I said truthfully.

He seemed satisfied, I thought, because he grunted.

"Good," he said. "Now, come in here."

He led me into a room, bare save for the trestle table in the centre, and drew back the sheet from the face of the thing that lay upon it.

"Now," he said triumphantly, "now, Campion, what d'you think of this?"

I said nothing at all. Lying on the table was the body of Pig Peters, Pig Peters unmistakable as Leo himself, and I knew without touching his limp, podgy hand that he could not have been dead more than twelve hours at the outside.

Yet in January...and this was June.

CHAPTER 2

Decent Murder

NOT UNNATURALLY THE whole thing was something of a shock to me and I suppose I stood staring at the corpse as though it were a beautiful view for some considerable time.

At last Leo grunted and cleared his throat.

"Dead, of course," he said, no doubt to recall my attention. "Poor feller. Damnable cad, though. Ought not to say it of a dead man, perhaps, but there you are. Truth must out."

Leo really talks like this. I have often thought that his conversation, taken down verbatim, might be worth looking at. Just then I was more concerned with the matter than the form, however, and I said, "You knew him, then?"

Leo grew red round the jawbone and his white moustache pricked up.

"I'd met the feller," he murmured, conveying that he

thought it a shameful admission. "Had a most unpleasant interview with him only last night, I don't mind telling you. Extremely awkward in the circumstances. Still, can't be helped. There it is."

Since there was a considerable spot of mystery in the business already I saw no point in overburdening Leo's mind by adding my little contribution to it just then.

"What was he calling himself?" I inquired with considerable guile.

Leo had very bright blue eyes which, like most soldiers', are of an almost startling innocence of expression.

"Masqueradin', eh?" he said. "Upon my soul, very likely! Never thought of it. Untrustworthy customer."

"I don't know anything," I said hastily. "Who is he, anyway?"

"Harris," he said unexpectedly and with contempt. "Oswald Harris. More money than was good for him and the manners of an enemy non-commissioned officer. Can't put it too strongly. Terrible feller."

I looked at the dead man again. Of course it was Pig all right: I should have known him anywhere—and it struck me then as odd that the boy should really be so very much the father of the man. It's a serious thought when you look at some children.

Still, there was Pig and he was dead again, five months after his funeral, and Leo was growing impatient.

"See the wound?" he demanded.

He has a gift for the obvious. The top of the carrotty head was stove in, sickeningly, like a broken soccer ball, and the fact that the skin was practically unbroken made it somehow even more distressing. It was such a terrific smash that it seemed incredible that any human arm could have delivered the blow. It looked to me as if he had been kicked through a felt hat by a cart-horse and I said so to Leo.

He was gratified.

"Damn nearly right, my boy," he said with comforting enthusiasm. "Remarkable thing. Don't mind admitting don't follow this deducin' business myself, but substitute an urn for a cart-horse and you're absolutely right. Remind me to tell Janet."

"An urn?"

"Geranium urn, stone," he explained airily. "Big so-called ornamental thing. Must have seen 'em, Campion. Sometimes have cherry pie in 'em. Madness to keep 'em on the parapet. Said so myself more than once."

I was gradually getting the thing straight. Apparently Pig's second demise had been occasioned by a blow from a stone flower-pot falling on him from a parapet. It seemed pretty final this time.

I looked at Leo. We were both being very decent and noncommittal, I thought.

"Any suggestion of foul play, sir?" I asked.

He hunched his shoulders and became very despondent.

"'Fraid so, my boy," he said at last. "No way out of it. Urn was one of several set all along the parapet. Been up to inspect 'em myself. All firm as the Rock of Gibraltar. Been there for years. Harris's urn couldn't have hopped off the ledge all by itself, don't you know. Must have been pushed by—er—human hands. Devilish situation in view of everything. Got to face it."

I covered Pig's body. I was sorry for him in a way, of course, but he seemed to have retained his early propensities for making trouble.

Leo sighed. "Thought you'd have to agree with me," he said.

I hesitated. Leo is not one of the great brains of the earth, but I could hardly believe that he had dragged me down from London to confirm his suspicion that Pig had died from a bang on the head. I took it that there was more to come—and there was, of course; no end of it, as it turned out.

Leo stubbed a bony forefinger into my shoulder.

"Like to have a talk with you, my boy," he said. "One or two private matters to discuss. Have to come out some time. We ought to go down to Halt Knights and have a look at things."

The light began to filter in.

"Was P—was Harris killed at Halt Knights?"

Leo nodded. "Poor Poppy! Decent little woman, you know, Campion. Never a suspicion of—er anything of this sort before."

"I should hope not," I said, scandalized, and he frowned at me.

"Some of these country clubs—" he began darkly.

"Not murder," I said firmly and he relapsed into despondency.

"Perhaps you're right," he agreed. "Let's go down there. Drop in for a drink before dinner."

As we went out to the car I considered the business. To understand Halt Knights is to know Kepesake, and Kepesake is a sort of county paradise. It is a big village, just far enough from a town and a main road to remain exclusive without having to be silly about it. It has a Norman church, a village cricket green with elms, three magnificent pubs, and a population of genuine country folk of proper independent views.

It lies in a gentle valley on the shores of an estuary and is protected by a ring of modest little estates all owned by dear good fellers, so Leo says. The largest of these estates is Halt Knights.

At one period there was a nobleman at the Knights who owned the whole village, which had been left him by an ancestress who had had it, so the name would suggest, from a boy-friend off to the Crusades. Changing times and incomes drove out the nobleman and his heirs; hence the smaller estates.

The house and some nine hundred acres of meadow and salting remained a millstone round somebody's neck until Poppy Bellew retired from the stage and, buying it up, transformed that part of it which had not collapsed into the finest hotel and country pub in the kingdom.

Being a naturally expansive person of untiring energy, she did not let the nine hundred acres worry her but laid down an eighteen hole golf course and reserved the rest for anything anyone might think of. It occurred to some intelligent person that there was a very fine point-to-point course there somewhere and at the time Pig got the urn on his head there had been four meetings there in each of five consecutive springs.

It was all very lazy and homely and comfortable. If anyone who looked as if he might spoil the atmosphere came along somehow Poppy lost him. It was really very simple. She wanted to keep open house and the people round about were willing to pay their own expenses, or that was how it seemed to work out.

Leo's story was interesting. I could understand Pig getting himself killed at Halt Knights, but not how he managed to stay there long enough for it to happen.

Meanwhile Leo had reached the car and was looking at Lugg with mistrust. Leo's ideas of discipline are military and Lugg's are not. I foresaw an impasse.

"Ah, Lugg," I said with forced heartiness, "I'm going to drive Sir Leo on to Halt Knights. You'd better go back to Highwaters. Take a bus or something."

Lugg stared at me and I saw rebellion in his eyes. His feet have been a constant source of conversation with him of late.

"A bus?" he echoed, adding "sir" as a belated afterthought as Leo's eyes fell upon him.

"Yes," I said foolishly. "One of those big green things. You must have seen them about."

He got out of the car heavily and with dignity and so far demeaned himself as to hold the door open for Leo, but me he regarded under fat white eyelids with a secret, contemplative expression.

"Extraordinary feller, your man," said Leo as we drove off. "Keep an eye on him, my dear boy. Save your life in the war?"

"Dear me, no!" I said in some astonishment. "Why?"

He blew his nose. "I don't know. Thought just crossed my mind. Now to this business, Campion. It's pretty serious and I'll tell you why." He paused and added so soberly that I started: "There are at least half a dozen good fellers, including myself, who were in more than half a mind to put that feller out of the way last night. One of us must have lost his head, don't you know. I'm being very frank with you, of course."

I pulled the car up by the side of the road. We were on the long straight stretch above the "Dog and Fowl."

"I'd like to hear about it," I said.

He came out with it quietly and damningly in his pleasant worried voice. It was an enlightening tale in view of the circumstances.

Two of the estates nearby had become vacant in the past year and each had been bought anonymously through a firm of London solicitors. No one thought much of it at the time but the blow had fallen about a week before our present conversation. Leo, going down to Halt Knights for a game of bridge and a drink, also had found the place in an uproar and Pig, of all people, installed. He was throwing his weight about and detailing his plans for the future of Kepesake, which included a hydro, a dog-racing track, and a cinema-dance-hall with special attractions to catch motorists from the none too far distant industrial town.

Taken on one side, Poppy had broken down and made a confession. Country ease and country hospitality had proven expensive, and she, not wishing to depress her clients, who were also her nearest and dearest friends, had accepted the generous mortgage terms which a delightful gentleman from London had arranged, only to find that his charming personality had been but the mask to cloak the odious Pig, who had decided to foreclose at the precise moment when a few outstanding bills had been paid with the greater part of the loan.

Leo, who justified his name if ever man did, had padded forth gallantly to the rescue. He roared round the district, collected a few good souls of his own kidney, held a meeting, formed a syndicate, and approached the entrenched Pig armed with money and scrupulously fair words.

From that point, however, he had met defeat. Pig was adamant. Pig had all the money he required. Pig wanted Kepesake—and a fine old silver sty he was going to make of it.

Leo's solicitor, summoned from Norwich, had confirmed his client's worst fears. Poppy had trusted the charming gentleman too well. Pig had an option to purchase.

Realizing that with money, Halt Knights, and the two adjoining estates Pig could lay waste Kepesake, and their hearts with it, Leo and his friends had tried other methods. As Leo pointed out, men will fight for their homes. There is a primitive love inspired by tree and field which can fire the most correct heart to flaming passion.

Two or three of Halt Knights' oldest guests were asked by Pig to leave. Leo and most of the others stolidly sat their ground, however, and talk was high but quiet, while plots abounded.

"And then this morning, don't you know," Leo finished mildly, "one of the urns on the parapet crashed down on the feller as he sat sleepin' in a deck-chair under the lounge window. Devilish awkward, Campion."

I let in the clutch and drove on without speaking. I thought of Kepesake and its gracious shadowy trees, its sweet meadows and clear waters, and thought what a howling shame it was. It belonged to these old boys and their children. It was their sanctuary, their little place of peace. If Pig wanted to make more money, why in heaven's name should he rot up Kepesake to do it? There are ten thousand other villages in England. Well, they'd saved it from Pig at any rate, or at least one of them had. So much looked painfully apparent.

Neither of us spoke until we turned in under the red Norman arch which is the main drive gate to the Knights. There Leo snorted.

"Another bounder!" he said explosively.

I looked at the little figure mincing down the drive towards us and all but let the car swerve on to the turf. I recognized him immediately, principally by the extraordinary sensation of dislike he aroused in me. He was a thoroughly unpleasant old fellow, affected and conceited, and the last time I had seen him he had been weeping ostentatiously into a handkerchief with an inch-wide black border at Pig's first funeral. Now he was trotting out of Halt Knights as if he knew the place and was very much at home there.

CHAPTER 3

"That's Where He Died"

HE LOOKED AT ME with interest and I think he placed me, for I was aware of two beady bright eyes peering at me from beneath Cairn eyebrows.

Leo, on the other hand, received a full salute from him, a wave of the panama delivered with one of those shrugs which attempt old-world grace and achieve the slightly sissy.

Leo gobbled and tugged perfunctorily at his own green tweed.

"More people know Tom Fool than Tom Fool knows," he confided to me in an embarrassed rumble and hurried on so quickly that I took it he did not want the man discussed, which was curious.

"I want you to be careful with Poppy," he said. "Charmin' little woman. Had a lot to put up with the last day or two.

Wouldn't like to see her browbeaten. Kid gloves, Campion. Kid gloves all the way."

I was naturally aggrieved. I have never been considered brutal, having if anything a mild and affable temperament.

"It's ten years since I beat a woman, sir," I said. Leo cocked an eye at me. Facetiae are not his line.

"Hope you never have," he said severely. "Your mother— dear sweet lady—wouldn't have bred a son who could. I'm worried about Poppy, Campion. Poor charmin' little woman."

I felt my eyebrows rise. The man who could visualize Poppy as a poor little woman must also, I felt, be able to think of her being actually ill-treated. I like Poppy. Charming she certainly is, but little—no. Leo was confusing the ideal with the conventional, and I might have told him so and mortally offended him had we not come through the trees at that moment to see the house awaiting us.

No English country house is worthy of the name if it is not breathtaking at half past six on a June evening, but Halt Knights is in a street by itself. It is long and low, with fine windows. Built of crushed strawberry brick, the Georgian front does not look out of place against the Norman ruins which rise up behind it and melt into the high chestnuts massed at the back.

As in many East Anglian houses the front door is at the side, so that the lawn can come right up to the house in front.

As we pulled up I was glad to see that the door was open as usual, though the place seemed deserted save for the embarrassed bobby in bicycle clips who stood on guard by the lintel.

I could not understand his acute discomfort until I caught the gleam of a pewter tankard among the candytuft at his feet. Poppy has a great understanding of the creature man.

I touched Leo on the shoulder and made a suggestion and he blinked at me.

"Oh all right, my boy. Make the examination first if you want to, by all means. This is where the feller was sittin'."

He led me round to the front of the house where the deck-chairs, looking flimsy and oddly Japanese in their bright colours, straggled along under the windows.

"The urn," he said.

I bent down and pulled aside the couple of sacks which had been spread over the exhibit. As soon as I saw it I understood his depression. It was a large stone basin about two and a half feet high and two feet across and was decorated with amorelli and pineapples. It must have weighed the best part of three hundredweight with the earth it contained, and while I could understand it killing Pig I was amazed that it had not smashed him to pulp. I said so to Leo and he explained.

"Would have done—would have done, my boy, but only the edge of the rim struck his head where it jutted over the back of the chair. He had a hat on, you know. There's the chair—nothing much to see."

He kicked aside another sack and we looked down at a pathetic heap of splintered framework and torn canvas. Leo shrugged his shoulders helplessly.

I walked a little way down the lawn and looked up at the parapet. It is one of those long strips of plastered stone which finish off the flat fronts of Georgian houses and always remind me of the topping of marzipan icing on a very good fruit cake. The little windows of the second floor sit behind it in the sugarloaf roof.

There were seven other urns set along the parapet at equal distances, and one significant gap. There was obviously nothing dangerous about them; they looked as if they had been there for ever.

We went towards the house.

"There's one thing I don't understand," I said. "Our murderer pal seems to have taken a tremendous risk. What an extremely dangerous thing to do."

Leo looked at me as though I had begun to gibber and I laboured on, trying to make myself clear.

"I mean," I said, "surely Harris wasn't sitting out here entirely alone? Someone might have come up to him to chat. The man who pushed the flowerpot over couldn't have made certain he was going to hit the right man unless he'd actually climbed out on the parapet to look first, which would have been lunatic."

Leo grew very red. "Harris was alone," he said. "He was sittin' out here when we turned up this mornin' and nobody felt like goin' to join him, don't you know. We left him where he was. He ignored us and no one felt like speakin' to him, so we all went inside. I was playin' a game of cards in the lounge through this window here when the infernal thing crashed down on him. You may think it childish," he added a little shamefacedly, "but there you are. The feller was an unmitigated tick."

I whistled. The clouds were blowing up.

"When you say 'all of you,' who do you mean?" I asked.

He looked wretched.

"About a dozen of us," he said. "All absolutely above suspicion. Let's go in."

As soon as we set foot on the stone flags of the entrance hall and sniffed the sweet cool fragrance of old wood and flowers which is the true smell of your good country house, Poppy appeared, fat, gracious, and welcoming as always.

"Why, ducky," she said as she took my hands, "how very

nice to see you. Leo, you're a lamb to send for him. Isn't it awful? Come and have a drink."

She piloted us down the broad stone corridor to the big white-panelled lounge with the deep, comfortable, chintz-covered chairs, chattering the whole time.

It is not easy to describe Poppy. She is over fifty, I suppose, with tight grey curls all over her head, a wide mouth, and enormous blue eyes. That is the easy part. The rest is more difficult. She exudes friendliness, generosity, and a sort of naive obstinacy. Her clothes are outrageous, vast flowery skirts and bodices embellished with sufficient frills to rig a frigate. However, they suit her personality if not her figure. You see her and you like her and that's all there is to it.

Leo was plainly batty about her.

"Such a horrid little man, Harris," she said as she gave me my whisky. "Has Leo told you all about him and me? How he tried to pinch the place… He has! Oh, well, that's all right. You see how it happened. Still, it's very wrong of someone, very wrong indeed—although, my dear, I'm sure they meant to be kind."

Leo spluttered. "Isn't she a *dear?*" he said.

"I'm not being silly, am I, Albert?" She looked at me appealingly. "I did tell them it was dangerous last night. I said quite distinctly 'This will lead to trouble' and of course it did."

I intercepted a startled glance from Leo and sat up with interest. Poppy turned on him.

"Haven't you told him?" she said. "Oh but you must. It's not fair."

Leo avoided my eyes. "I was comin' to that," he said. "I've only had Campion down here for half an hour."

"You were trying to shield them," said Poppy devastatingly, "and that's no good. When we've got the truth," she added naively, "then we can decide how much we're going to tell."

Leo looked scandalized and would have spoken but she forestalled him.

"It was like this," she said confidingly, giving my arm a friendly but impersonal pat. "Two or three of the more hearty old pets hatched up a plot last night. They were going to get Harris drunk and friendly first and then they were going to put the whole thing to him as man to man and in a burst of good fellowship he was going to sign a document they'd had prepared, relinquishing the option or whatever it is."

She paused and eyed me dubiously, as well she might, I thought. As my face did not change she came a little nearer.

"I didn't approve," she said earnestly. "I told them it was silly and in a way not quite honest. But they said Harris hadn't been honest with us and of course that was right too, so they sat up in here with him last night. It might have been all right only instead of getting friendly he got truculent, as some people do, and while they were trying to get him beyond that stage he passed out altogether and they had to put him to bed. This morning he had a terrible hangover and went to sleep it off on the lawn. He hadn't moved all the morning when that beastly thing fell on him."

"Awkward," murmured Leo. "Devilish awkward."

Poppy gave me the names of the conspirators. They were all eminently respectable people who ought to have known a great deal better. It sounded to me as if everybody's uncle had gone undergraduate again and I might have said so in a perfectly friendly way had not Poppy interrupted me.

"Leo's Inspector—such a nice man; he's hoping to get promotion, he tells me—has been through the servants with a toothcomb and hasn't found anything, not even a brain, the poor ducks! I'm afraid there's going to be a dreadful scandal. It must be one of the visitors, you see, and I only have such dear people."

I said nothing, for at that moment a pudding-faced maid, who certainly did not look as though she had sufficient intelligence to drop an urn or anything else on the right unwanted guest, came in to say that if there was a Mr. Campion in the house he was wanted on the telephone.

I took it for granted it was Janet and I went along to the hall with a certain pleasurable anticipation.

As soon as I took up the receiver, however, the exchange said brightly: "London call."

Considering I had left the city unexpectedly two hours before with the intention of going to Highwaters, and no one in the world but Lugg and Leo knew that I had come to Halt Knights, I thought there must be some mistake and I echoed her.

"Yes, that's right. London call," she repeated with gentle patience. "Hold on. You're through…"

I held on for some considerable time.

"Hullo," I said at last. "Hullo. Campion here."

Still there was no reply, only a faint sigh, and the someone at the other end hung up. That was all.

It was an odd little incident, rather disturbing.

Before going back to the others I wandered upstairs to the top floor to have a look at the parapet. No one was about and most of the doors stood open, so that I had very little difficulty in finding the spot where Pig's urn had once stood.

It had been arranged directly in front of a box-room window and must, I thought, have obscured most of the light. When I came to look at the spot I saw that any hopeful theory I might have formed concerning a clumsy pigeon or a featherbrained cat was out of the question. The top of the parapet was covered with lichen save for the square space where the foot of the urn had stood. This was clear and brown save for the bodies of a few dead bugs of the kind one gets under stones, and in the centre of it there was a little slot, some three inches wide and two deep, designed to hold some sort of stone peg incorporated in the bottom of the urn all for safety's sake.

There was no question of the fall being accidental, therefore. Someone both strong and determined must have lifted the heavy thing up before pushing it out.

There was nothing unusual about the vacant space, as far as I could see, save that the lichen at the edge of the parapet was slightly damp. How important that was I did not dream.

I went down again to the lounge. I am a naturally unobtrusive person and I suppose I came in quietly, because neither Leo nor Poppy seemed to hear me, and I caught his words, which were loud and excited.

"My dear lady, believe me, I don't want to butt into your private affairs—nothing's farther from my mind—but it was a natural question. Hang it all, Poppy, the feller was a bounder, and there he was striding out of this place as though it belonged to him. However, don't tell me who he was if you'd rather not."

Poppy faced him. Her cheeks were pink and her eyes were bright with tears of annoyance.

"He came from the village to—to sell some tickets for a—a whist drive," she said, all in one breath, and I, looking at her, wondered if she could have been such a very great actress after all, since she couldn't tell a lie better than that.

Then, of course, I realized who they were talking about.

CHAPTER 4

Among the Angels

I COUGHED DISCREETLY, and Leo turned round to glance at me guiltily. He looked miserable.

"Ah!" he said absently, but with a valiant attempt to make normal conversation. "Ah, Campion, not bad news, I hope?"

"No news at all," I said truthfully.

"Oh, well, that's good. That's good, my boy," he bellowed suddenly, getting up and clapping me on the shoulder with unnecessary fervour. "No news is good news. We always say that, don't we? Well, Poppy, ought to go now, m'dear. People to dinner, you know. Good-bye. Come along, Campion. Glad you had good news."

The old boy was frankly blethering, and I was sorry for him. Poppy was still annoyed. Her cheeks were very pink and her eyes were tearful.

Leo and I went out.

I made him come on to the lawn again where I had another look at the urn. The peg was intact. It protruded nearly two and a half inches from the flat surface of the stand.

Leo was very thoughtful when I pointed it out to him, but his mind could hardly have been on his work, for I had to explain the primitive arrangement to him twice before he saw any significance in it.

As we drove off under the trees he looked at me.

"Kittle-cattle," he said sadly.

We drove back on to the main road in silence. I was glad of the spot of quiet because I took it that a little constructive thinking was overdue. I am not one of these intellectual sleuths, I am afraid. My mind does not work like an adding machine, taking the facts in neatly one by one and doing the work as it goes along. I am more like the bloke with the sack and spiked stick. I collect all the odds and ends I can see and turn out the bag at the lunch hour.

So far, I had netted one or two things. I had satisfied myself that Pig had been murdered; that is to say, whoever had killed him had done so intentionally, but not, I thought, with much premeditation. This seemed fairly obvious, since it was not reasonable to suppose that anyone could have insisted on him sitting just in that one spot, or made absolutely certain that he would stay there long enough to receive the urn when it came.

Considering the matter, I fancied some impulsive fellow had happened along to find the stage set, as it were; Pig sitting, porcine and undesirable, under the flower pot, and, not being able to curb the unworthy instinct, had trotted upstairs and done the necessary shoving all in the first fierce flush of inspiration.

Having arrived at this point, it struck me that the actual

identification of the murderer must depend upon a process of elimination after an examination of alibis, and this, I thought, was definitely a job for the Inspector. After all, he was the young hopeful out for promotion.

The real trouble, I foresaw, would be the question of proof. Since finger-prints on the rough cast would be too much to hope for, and an eye-witness would have come forward before now, it was in pinning the crime down that I imagined the real snag would arise.

Perhaps I ought to mention here that at that moment I was absolutely wrong. I was wrong not only about the position of the snag but about everything else as well. However, I had no idea of it then. I leant back in the Lagonda with Leo at my side, and drove through the yellow evening light thinking of Pig and his two funerals, past and present.

At that time, and I was hopelessly mistaken, of course, I was inclined to think that Pig's murderer was extraneous to the general scheme. The clever young gentleman from London innocently looked forward to a nice stimulating civil mystery with the criminal already under lock and key in the mortuary, and this in spite of the telephone call and Poppy's unpleasant visitor. Which proves to me now that the balmy country air had gone to my head.

I was sorry for Leo and Poppy and the overzealous old gentlemen who had come so disastrously to the aid of Halt Knights. I sympathized with them over the scandal and the general rumpus. But at that moment I did not think that the murder itself was by any means the most exciting part of the situation.

Of course, had I known of the other odds and ends that the gods had in the bag for us, had I realized that the unpleasant

Old Person with the Scythe was just sitting up in the garden resting on his laurels and getting his breath for the next bit of gleaning, I should have taken myself in hand, but I honestly thought the fireworks were over and that I had come in at the end of the party and not, as it turned out, at the beginning.

As we drove down the narrow village street past "The Swan," I asked Leo a question as casually as I could.

"D'you know Tethering, sir?" I said. "There's a nursing home there, isn't there?"

"Eh?" He roused himself with a jerk from his unhappy meditations. "Tethering? Nursin' home? Oh, yes, excellent place—excellent. Run by young Brian Kingston. A good feller. Very small, though, very small—the nursin' home, not Kingston. You'll like him. Big feller. Dear chap. Comin' to dinner tonight. Vicar's comin' too," he added as an afterthought. "Just the five of us. Informal, you know."

Naturally, I was interested.

"Has Kingston had the place long?"

Leo blinked at me. He seemed to wish I wouldn't talk.

"Oh, several years. Father used to practise there years ago. Left the son a large house and he, bein' enterprisin' chap, made a goin' concern of it. Good doctor—wonderful doctor. Cured my catarrh."

"You know him well, then?" I asked, feeling sorry to intrude upon his thoughts but anxious to get on with the inquiry.

Leo sighed. "Fairly well," he said. "Well as one knows anyone, don't you know. Funny thing, I was playin' a hand with him and two other fellers this mornin' when that confounded urn fell on that bounder outside and made all this trouble. Came right down past the window where we were sittin'. Terrible thing. "

"What were you playing? Bridge?"

Leo looked scandalized. "Before lunch? No, my dear boy. Poker. Wouldn't play bridge before lunch. Poker, that's what it was. Kingston had a queen-pot and we were settlin' up, thinkin' about lunch, when there was a sort of shadow past the window, and then a sort of thud that wasn't an ordinary thud. Damned unpleasant. I didn't like the look of him, did you? Looked a dangerous fellow, I thought, the sort of feller one'd set a dog on instinctively."

"Who?" I said, feeling I was losing the thread of the argument.

Leo grunted. "That feller we met in the drive at Poppy's place. Can't get him out of my mind."

"I think I've seen him before," I said.

"Oh?" Leo looked at me suspiciously. "Where? Where was that?"

"Er—at a funeral somewhere," I said, not wishing to be more explicit.

Leo blew his nose. "Just where you'd expect to see him," he said unreasonably, and we turned into the drive of Highwaters.

Janet came hurrying down the steps as we pulled up.

"Oh, darling, you're so late," she murmured to Leo and, turning to me, held out her hand. "Hello, Albert," she said, a little coldly, I thought.

I can't describe Janet as I saw her then. She was, and is, very lovely.

I still like her.

"Hello," I said flatly, and added idiotically because I felt I ought to say something else: "Give us to drink, Ambrosia, and sweet Barm—"

She turned away from me and addressed Leo.

"You really must go and dress, pet. The Vicar's here, all of a twitter, poor boy. The whole village is seething with excitement, he says, and Miss Dusey sent up to say that 'The Marquis' is full of newspaper men. She wants to know if it's all right. Has anything turned up?"

"No, no, m'dear." Leo spoke absently and kissed her, unexpectedly, I felt sure.

He seemed to think the caress a little surprising himself, for he coughed as though to cover, or at least to excuse it, and hurried into the house, leaving her standing, dark-haired and attractive, on the step beside me.

"He's worried, isn't he?" she said under her breath, and then went on, as though she had suddenly remembered who I was, "I'm afraid you must go and dress at once. You've only got ten minutes. Leave the car here and I'll send someone to take it round."

I have known Janet, on and off, for twenty-three years. When I first saw her she was bald and pinkly horrible. I was almost sick at the sight of her, and was sent out into the garden until I had recovered my manners. Her formality both hurt and astonished me, therefore.

"All right," I said, anxious to be accommodating at all costs. "I won't wash."

She looked at me critically. She has very fine eyes, like Leo's, only larger.

"I should," she said gently. "You show the dirt, don't you?—like a white fur."

I took her hand. "Friends, eh?" I said anxiously. She laughed, but not very naturally.

"My dear, of course. Oh, by the way, your friend called

at about half past six, but didn't stay. I said I expected you for dinner."

"Lugg," I said apprehensively, a great light dawning upon me. "What's he done?"

"Oh, not *Lugg*." She spoke with contempt. "I *like* Lugg. Your girl-friend."

The situation was getting out of hand.

"It's all a lie," I said. "There is no other woman. Did she leave a name?"

"She did." There was grimness and I thought spite in Janet's tone. "Miss Effie Rowlandson."

"Never heard of her," I said honestly. "Was she a nice girl?"

"No," said Janet explosively, and ran into the house.

I went into Highwaters alone. Old Pepper, pottering about in the hall doing the odd jobs that butlers do, seemed pleased to see me, and I was glad of that. After a gracious though formal greeting, "A letter for you, sir," he said, in the same way as a man might say, "I am happy to present you with a medal."

"It came this morning, and I was about to readdress it and send it on to you, when Sir Leo informed me that we were to expect you this evening."

He retired to his private cubby-hole at the back of the hall and returned with an envelope.

"You are in your usual room, sir, in the east wing," he said, as he came up. "I will send George with your cases immediately. It wants but seven minutes before the gong."

I glanced at the envelope in my hand as he was sauntering off, and I suppose I hiccuped or something, for he glanced round at me with kindly concern.

"I beg your pardon, sir?"

"Nothing, Pepper," I said, confirming his worst fears, and, tearing open the envelope, I read the second anonymous letter as I went up to my room. It was as neatly typed and precisely punctuated as the first had been, quite a pleasure to read.

"O," saith the owl. "Oho," sobbeth the frog. "O-oh," mourneth the worm. "Where is Peters that was promised us?"

The Angel weepeth behind golden bars. His wings cover his face. "Piero," weepeth the Angel.

Why should these things be? Who was he to disturb the heavens?

Consider, o consider the lowly mole. His small hands are sore and his snout bleedeth.

CHAPTER 5

Nice People

"IT'S THE NATURE-NOTE *motif* I find confusing," I confided to Lugg as I dressed. "See any point in it at all?"

He threw the letter aside and smiled at me with unexpected sheepishness. Sentiment glistened all over his face.

"Pore little mole," he said.

I gaped at him, and he had the grace to look abashed. He recovered this truculence almost at once, however.

"That walk," he began darkly. "I'm glad you've come in. I've been waitin' to talk to you. What do you think I am? A perishin' centipede? Green bus, my old sock!"

"You're getting old," I said offensively. "See if your mental faculties have failed as far as your physique has deteriorated. I have four minutes to get down to the dining-room. Does that letter convey anything to you or not? It was sent here. It arrived this morning."

The dig touched him and his great white face was reproachful as he reread the note, his lips moving soundlessly.

"A owl, a frog, a worm, and an angel are all upset because they can't find this 'ere Peters," he said at last. "That's clear, ain't it?"

"Dazzlingly," I agreed. "And it would suggest that the writer knew Peters was not dead, which is interesting, because he is. The fellow I've been to see in the mortuary is—or rather was—Peters himself. He died this morning."

Lugg eyed me. "'Avin a game?" he inquired coldly.

I considered him with disgust as I struggled with my collar, and presently he continued without help, making an obvious effort to get his mind working.

"This mornin'? Reelly?" he said. "Died, did he? What of?"

"Flower pot on the head, with intent."

"Done in? Reelly?" Lugg returned to the note. "Oh, well then, this is clear, ain't it? The bloke 'oo wrote this knew you was always anxious to snuff round a bit of blood, doin' the rozzers out of their rightful, and 'e kindly give you the tip to come along 'ere as fast as you could so's you wouldn't miss nothink."

"Yes, well, you're offensive, muddle-headed, and vulgar," I said with dignity.

"Vulgar?" he echoed in sudden concern. "Not vulgar, cock. I may say what I mean, but I'm never vulgar."

He considered a moment.

"Rozzers," he announced with triumph. "You're right, rozzers is common. P'lice officers."

"You make me sick," I said truthfully. "The point you seem to have missed is that Peters died this morning, and that letter was posted to me at this address from central London some time before seven o'clock last night."

He took in the facts and surprised me by getting up.

"'Ere," he said, "see what this means? The bloke 'oo wrote you last night *knoo* Peters was goin' to die today."

I hesitated. It was the first time I had felt the genuine trickle up the spine. Meanwhile he went on complaining.

"You've done it again," he mourned. "In spite of all I've done for you, here you are mixed up in the first bit of cheap mud that comes along. Lumme! You don't 'ave to whistle for it, even. It flies to you."

I looked at him. "Lugg," I said, "these words are in the nature of a prophecy. The puff paste has a sausage inside it, after all."

The gong forestalled him, but his comment followed me as I hurried to the door.

"Botulistic, most likely," he said.

I arrived in the dining-room with half a second to spare, and Pepper regarded me with affection, which was more than Janet did, I was sorry to see.

Leo was talking to a slim black back in a clerical dinner jacket, and I sat down to find myself beside the pleasant-looking person with whom I had chatted at Pig's Tethering funeral.

He recognized me with a pleasing show of warmth, and laughed at me with deep lazy grey eyes.

"Always in at the death?" he murmured.

We introduced ourselves, and I liked his manner. He was a big fellow, older than I was, with a certain shyness which was attractive. We chatted for some moments, and Janet joined us, and it was not until some minutes later that I became aware of someone hating me.

It is one of those odd but unmistakable sensations one

experiences sometimes on buses or at private dinners, and I looked across the table to observe a young cleric whom I had never seen before regarding me with honest hostility. He was one of those tall, bony ascetics with high-red cheek and wrist bones, and the humourless round black eyes of the indignant-hearted.

I was so taken back that I smiled at him foolishly, and Leo introduced us.

He turned out to be the Reverend Philip Smedley Bathwick, newly appointed to the parish of Kepesake. I could not understand his unconcealed hatred, and was rather hurt by it until I saw him glance at Janet. Then I began to follow him. He positively goggled at her, and I might have felt sorry for him had it not been for something personal that there is no need to go into here.

He was doubly unfortunate, as it happened, because Leo monopolized him. As soon as we were safely embarked on the fish the old man bellowed, as he always does when he fancies the subject needs finesse: "That fellow we were talking about before dinner; where d'you say he's staying?"

"At Mrs. Thatcher's, sir. Do you know the woman? She has a little cottage below 'The Swan.'"

Bathwick had a good voice, but there was a tremor in it which I put down to his suppressed anxiety to listen to the conversation at our end of the table.

Leo was not giving him any respite.

"Oh, I know old Mrs. Thatcher," he said. "One of the Jepson family on Blucher's Hill. A good woman. What's she doin' with a feller like that in the house? Can't understand it, Bathwick."

"She lets rooms, sir." Bathwick's eyes wandered to Janet

and away again, as if the sight hurt him. "This Mr. Hayhoe has only been in the village a little under a week."

"Heigh-ho?" said Leo. "Idiotic name. Probably false."

As usual when he is irritated he blared at the unfortunate young man, who gaped at him.

"Hayhoe is a fairly common name, sir," Bathwick ventured.

"Heigh-ho?" repeated Leo, looking at him as if he were demented. "I don't believe it. When you're as old as I am, Bathwick, you'll give up trying to be funny. This is a serious time, my dear feller, a serious time."

Bathwick grew crimson about the ears at the injustice, but he controlled himself and glowered silently. It was a ridiculous incident, but it constituted, I submit, the whole reason why Leo considers Bathwick a facetious ass to this day, which is pity, of course, for a more serious-minded cove was never born.

At the time I was more interested in the information than the man, however, and I turned to Kingston.

"D'you remember a fantastic old man in a top hat weeping into an immense mourning handkerchief at that funeral at your place last winter?" I said. "That was Hayhoe."

He blinked at me. "Peters' funeral? No, I don't think I remember him. There was an odd sort of girl there, I know, and—"

He paused, and I saw a kind of excitement come into his eyes.

"—I say!" he said.

We were all looking at him, and he became embarrassed, and struggled to change the subject. As soon as the others were talking again, however, he turned to me.

"I've just thought of something," he said, his voice as eager as a boy's. "It may be useful. We'll have a chat after dinner, if you don't mind. You didn't know that fellow Peters well, did you?"

"Not intimately," I said guardedly.

"He wasn't a nice chap," he said and added, lowering his voice, "I believe I'm on to something. Can't tell you here."

He met my eyes, and my heart warmed to him. I like enthusiasm for the chase, or it's an inhuman business.

We did not have an opportunity to talk immediately we broke up, however, because the Inspector in charge of the case came to see Leo while the port was still in circulation, and he excused himself.

Left with Bathwick, Kingston and I had our hands full. He was a red-hot innovator, we discovered. He spoke with passion of the insanitary condition of the thatched cottages and the necessity of bringing culture into the life of the average villager, betraying, I thought, a lack of acquaintance with either the thatched cottage or, of course, the villager in question, who, as every countryman knows, does not exist.

Kingston and I were trying to convince him that the whole point of a village is that it is a sufficiently scattered community for a man to call his soul his own in it without seriously inconveniencing his neighbour, when Pepper arrived to ask me if I would join Sir Leo in the gun-room.

I went into the fine old chamber on the first floor, where Leo does both his writing and his gun cleaning with impartial enthusiasm, to find him sitting at his desk. In front of him was an extremely attractive soul enjoying a glass of whisky. Leo introduced him.

"Inspector Pussey, Campion, my boy. Able feller. Been workin' like a nigger all day."

I liked Pussey on sight; anyone would.

He was lank and loose-jointed, and had one of those slightly comic faces which are both disarming and endearing, and it was evident that he regarded Leo with that amused affection and admiration which is the bedrock of the co-operation between man and master in rural England.

When I arrived they were both perturbed. I took it that the affair touched them both nearly. It was murder in the home meadow, so to speak. But there was more to it even than that, I found.

"Extraordinary thing, Campion," Leo said when Pepper had closed the door behind me. "Don't know what to make of it at all. Pussey here assures me of the facts, and he's a good man. Every reason to trust him every time."

I glanced at the Inspector. He looked proudly puzzled, I thought, like a spaniel which has unexpectedly retrieved a dodo. I waited, and Leo waved to Pussey to proceed. He smiled at me disarmingly.

"It's a king wonder, sir," he said, and his accent was soft and broad. "Seems like we've made a mistake somewhere, but where that is I can't tell you, nor I can't now. We spent the whole day, my man and I, questioning of people, and this evening we got 'em all complete, as you'd say."

"And no one but Sir Leo has a decent alibi?" I said sympathetically. "I know…"

"No, sir." Pussey did not resent my interruption; rather he welcomed it. He had a natural flair for the dramatic. "No, sir. Everyone has their alibi, and a good one, sir. The kitchen was eating of its dinner at the time of the accident, and everyone was present, even the garden boy. Everyone else in the house was in the lounge or in the bar that leads out of it, and has two or three other gentlemen's word to prove it. There was no strangers in the place, if you see what I mean, sir. All the gentlemen who called on Miss Bellew this morning came for a purpose, as you might say. They all knew each other well. One of 'em couldn't have gone off and done it unless..."

He paused, getting very red.

"Unless what?" said Leo anxiously. "Go on, my man. Don't stand on ceremony. We're in lodge here. Unless what?"

Pussey swallowed.

"Unless *all the other gentlemen knew,* sir," he said, and hung his head.

CHAPTER 6

Departed Pig

THERE WAS AN AWKWARD pause for a moment, not unnaturally. Pussey remained dumb-stricken by his own temerity, I observed a customary diffidence, and Leo appeared to be struggling for comprehension.

"Eh!" he said at last. "Conspiracy, eh?"

Pussey was sweating. "Don't hardly seem that could be so, sir," he mumbled unhappily.

"I don't know..." Leo spoke judicially. "I don't know, Pussey. It's an idea. It's an idea. And yet, don't you know, it couldn't have been so in this case. They would all have had to be in it, don't you see, and *I was there.*"

It was a sublime moment. Leo spoke simply and with that magnificent innocence which is as devastating as it is blind. Pussey and I sighed with relief. The old boy had swept away the slender supports of fact and left us with a miracle, but it was worth it.

Leo continued to consider the case.

"No," he said at last. "No. Impossible. Quite impossible. We'll have to think of something else, Pussey. We'll go over the alibis together. Maybe there's a loophole somewhere; you never know."

They settled down to work and I, not wishing to interfere in the Inspector's province, drifted off to find Kingston. I discovered him in the drawing-room with Janet and Bathwick, who stiffened and bristled as I came in. I wished he wouldn't. I am not over-sensitive, I hope, but his violent dislike embarrassed me, and I offered him a cigarette on the gift principle. He refused it.

Kingston was as keen to chat as I was, and he suggested a cigar on the terrace. In any other drawing-room, with the possible exception of Great-aunt Caroline's at Cambridge, such a remark might have sounded stilted or at least consciously period, but Highwaters is that sort of house. The late Lady Pursuivant liked her furniture gilt and her porcelain by the ton.

I saw Bathwick shoot him a glance of dog-like gratitude which enhanced my sense of injustice, while Janet smouldered at me across the hearthrug.

We went out through the french windows on to as fine a marble terrace as any you'd find in Hollywood today, and Kingston took my arm.

"I say," he began, "that chap Peters..."

It took me back years to the little patch of grass behind the chapel at school and old Guffy taking me by the arm, with the same words uttered in exactly the same tone of mingled excitement and outrage.

"That chap Peters..."

"Yes?" I said encouragingly.

Kingston hesitated. "This is the nature of a confession," he began unexpectedly, and I fancy I stared at him, for he coloured and laughed. "Oh, I didn't rob the blighter," he said. "But I took down his will for him. That's what I wanted to talk to you about. He came down to my place to recuperate after appendicitis, you know. He made the arrangements himself by letter, and on the way down he picked up a chill and developed roaring pneumonia and died in spite of everything. He came to me because I was fairly inexpensive, you know. Someone in the district recommended him, he said, and mentioned a chap I knew slightly. Well, when he was very ill he had a lucid period, and he sent for me and said he wanted to make a will. I wrote it down, and he signed it."

Kingston paused and fidgeted.

"I'm telling you this because I know about you," he went on at last. "I've heard about you from Janet, and I know Sir Leo called you down on this Harris business. Well, Campion, as a matter of fact, I altered the will a bit."

"Did you though?" I said foolishly.

He nodded. "Not in substance, of course," he said; "but in form. I had to. As he dictated it it ran something like this: 'To that unspeakable bounder and unjailed crook, my brother, born Henry Richard Peters—whatever he may be calling himself now—I leave all I possess at the time of my death, including everything that may accrue to my estate after I die. I do this not because I like him, am sorry for him, or sympathize in any way with any nefarious business in which he may be engaged, but simply because he is the son of my mother, and I know of no one else.'"

Kingston hesitated, and regarded me solemnly in the moonlight.

"I didn't think it was decent," he said. "A thing like that can cause a lot of trouble. So I cleaned up the wording a bit. I simply made it clear that Mr. Peters wanted everything to go to his brother, and left it at that. He signed it and died."

He smoked for a moment or so in silence, and I waited for him to continue.

"As soon as I saw Harris he reminded me of someone," he said, "and tonight at dinner, when you reminded me of that funeral, I realized who it was. Peters and Harris had a great deal in common. They were made of the same sort of material, if you see what I mean, and had the same colouring. Peters was larger and had more fat on him, but the more I think about it the stronger the likeness becomes. You see what I'm driving at, Campion? This man Harris may well be the legatee's brother."

He laughed apologetically.

"Now I've said it it doesn't sound so very exciting," he said.

I did not answer him at once. I knew perfectly well that the Peters in the mortuary was my Peters, and if there was a brother in the business, I took it that it was he who had been Kingston's patient. It confirmed my earlier suspicions that Pig had been up to something characteristically fishy before retribution in the flower-pot had overtaken him.

"I sent the will along to his solicitors," Kingston continued. "I took all instructions about the funeral and so on from them, and they paid my account. I've got their name at home; I'll let you have it. Tomorrow morning do?"

I assured him it would, and he went on:

"I was down at the Knights this morning when it happened," he said, not without a certain pride. "We were playing poker. I'd just netted a queen-pot when I heard the thud and we all rushed out. There was nothing to be done, of course. Have you seen the body?"

"Yes," I said. "I haven't examined it yet. Was that the first time you'd seen Harris?"

"Oh, Lord, no! He's been there all the week. I've had to go along there every day to see Flossie Gage, one of the maids. She's had jaundice. I didn't talk to Harris much because—well, none of us did, you know. He was an offensive type. That incident with Bathwick showed you the type he was."

"Bathwick?"

"Oh, didn't you hear about that?" Kingston warmed to me. Like most country doctors he relished a spot of gossip. "It had its humorous side in a way. Bathwick is an earnest soul, as you may have noticed."

I agreed, and he chuckled and hurried on:

"Harris talked about a dance hall and a bathing beach he was going to build on that bit of land which runs down to the creek on the far side of the cricket pitch. Bathwick heard the gossip and was appalled by it. It didn't fit into his own scheme for Kepesake's development, which is more on welfare lines— communal kitchens and superintended crèches, and so on. He rushed down to see Harris in a panic, and I believe there was a grand scene. Harris had a sort of sense of humour and took a delight in teasing old Bathwick, who has none. They were in the lounge at the Knights, and Bill Duchesney and one or two other people were there, so Harris had an audience and let himself go. Bill told me Bathwick went off at last with his eyes bulging. Harris had promised him dancing houris, secret casinos, and God knows what else, until the poor chap saw his dream yokel walking straight out of the church clinic on one side of the road into the jaws of hell on the other. Bill tried to soothe the Vicar, I believe, but he said he was scared out of his wits and shocked to the marrow. You see the sort of fellow Harris was. He liked to show off. There was no need for him to tease old Bathwick, who'd be quite a good chap if he wasn't so solemn. However, that's not the point. The question is, who killed Harris? I'll bring down that solicitor's name, and any papers I can find first thing in the morning, shall I?"

"I wish you would," I said trying not to sound too eager. "Thanks for telling me."

"Not at all. I wish I could be really helpful. It's so seldom anything happens down here." He laughed awkwardly. "That's a bit naïve, isn't it?" he murmured. "But you've no idea how dull the country is for a fairly intelligent man, Campion."

We went back to the drawing-room. Janet and Bathwick were listening to the wireless, but she got up and switched it off as we appeared, and Bathwick sighed audibly at the sight of me.

Leo looked in after a bit, but he was plainly preoccupied, and he excused himself soon after. Not unnaturally the party broke up early. Kingston went home, taking the reluctant and smouldering cleric with him, and Janet and I wandered out on the terrace. It was warm and moonlit and rather exotic, what with night-scented stocks in the garden below and nightingales in the ilex.

"Albert…" said Janet.

"Yes?"

"You've some very peculiar friends, haven't you?"

"Oh, you meet all kinds of people at school," I said defensively, my mind still clinging to Peters. "It's like knowing a lot of eggs. You can't tell which one is going to grow into something definitely offensive."

She drew a long breath and her eyes glinted in the faint light.

"I didn't know you went to a co-ed," she said witheringly. "That accounts for you, I suppose."

"In a way," I agreed mildly. "I remember Miss Marshall. What a topping Head she was, to be sure. Such a real little sport on the hockey field. Such a demon for impositions. Such a regular little whirlwind with the birch."

"Shut up," said Janet unreasonably. "How d'you like Bathwick?"

"A dear fellow," I said dutifully. "Where does he live?"

"At the Vicarage, just behind the Knights. Why?"

"Has he a nice garden?"

"Quite good. Why?"

"Does his garden adjoin the Knights' garden?"

"The vicarage garden runs up to the chestnut copse at the back of Poppy's place. Why?"

"I like to know a man's background," I said. "He's rather keen on you, isn't he?"

She did not answer me, and I fancied she considered the question to be in bad taste. To my astonishment I felt her shiver at my side.

"Albert," she said in a very small voice, "do you know who did this beastly murder?"

"No, not yet."

"You think you'll find out?" She was almost whispering.

"Yes," I said. "I'll find out."

She put her hand in mine. "Leo's very fond of Poppy," she murmured.

I held her hand closely. "Leo has no more idea who killed Harris than a babe unborn," I said.

She shivered again. "That makes it worse, doesn't it? It'll be such a dreadful shock for him when he—he has to know."

"Poppy?" I said.

Janet clung to my arm. "They'd all shield her, wouldn't they?" she said unsteadily. "After all, she had most to lose. Go back to Town, Albert. Give it up. Don't find out."

"Forget it," I said. "Forget it for now."

We walked on in silence for a little. Janet wore a blue dress and I said I liked it. She also wore her hair in a knot low on her neck, and I said I liked that, too.

After a while she paid me a compliment. She said I was an eminently truthful person, and she was sorry to have doubted my word in a certain matter of the afternoon.

I forgave her readily, not to say eagerly. We turned back towards the french windows and had just decided not to go in after all, when something as unforeseen as it was unfortunate occurred. Pepper came out, blowing gently. He begged our pardons, he said, but a Miss Effie Rowlandson had called to see Mr. Campion and he had put her in the breakfast-room.

CHAPTER 7

The Girl Friend

As I FOLLOWED Pepper through the house, I ventured to question him.

"What's she like, Pepper?"

He turned and eyed me with a glance which conveyed clearly that he was an old man, an experienced man, and that dust did not affect his eyesight.

"The young woman informed me that she was a great friend of yours, sir, which was why she took the liberty of calling on you so late." He spoke sadly, intimating that the rebuke hurt him as much as it did me. He opened the breakfast-room door.

"Yoo-hoo!" said someone inside.

Pepper withdrew and Miss Effie Rowlandson rose to meet me.

"O-oh!" she said, glancing up at me under fluttering lashes, "you're not really, truly cross, are you?"

I am afraid I looked at her blankly. She was petite, blonde, and girlish, with starry eyes and the teeth of toothpaste advertisements. Her costume was entirely black save for a long white quill in her hat, and the general effect lay somewhere between Hamlet and Aladdin.

"O-oh, you don't remember me," she said. "O-oh, how awful of me to have come! I made sure you'd remember me. I am a silly little fool, aren't I?"

She conveyed that I was a bit of a brute, but that she did not blame me, and life was like that.

"Perhaps you've got hold of the wrong man?" I suggested helpfully.

"O-oh no…" Again her lashes fluttered at me. "I remember you—at the funeral, you know." She lowered her voice modestly on the last words.

Suddenly she came back to me with a rush. She was the girl at Peters's funeral. Why I should have forgotten her and remembered the old man, I do not know, save that I recollect feeling that she was not the right person to stare at.

"Ah, yes," I said slowly. "I do remember now."

She clapped her hands and squealed delightedly.

"I knew you would. Don't ask me why, but I just knew it. I'm like that sometimes. I just know things."

At this point the conversation came to an abrupt deadlock. I was not at my best, and she stood looking at me, a surprisingly shrewd expression in her light grey eyes.

"I knew you'd help me," she added at last.

I was more than ever convinced that I was not her man, and was debating how to put it when she made a surprising statement.

"He trampled on me," she said. "I don't know when I've been so mistaken in a man. Still, a girl does make mistakes, doesn't she, Mr. Campion? I see I made a mistake in saying I was such an old friend of yours when we'd only met once—or really only just looked at each other. I know that now. I wouldn't do it again."

"Miss Rowlandson," I said, "why have you come? I—er—I have a right to know," I added stalwartly, trying to keep in the picture.

She peered at me. "O-oh, you're hard, aren't you?" she said. "All men are hard, aren't they? They're not all like him, though. O-oh, he was hard! Still," she added, with a wholly unconvincing attempt at gallant restraint, "I ought not to talk about him like that, did I, when he's dead—if he *is* dead. Is he?"

"Who?"

She giggled. "You're cautious, aren't you? Are all detectives cautious? I like a man to be cautious. Roly Peters, of course. I used to call him Roly-Poly. That used to make him cross. You'd never guess how cross that used to make him. Poor Roly-Poly! It's wrong to laugh when he's dead—if he *is* dead. Do you know?"

"My dear girl," I said. "We went to his funeral, didn't we?"

I suppose I spoke sharply, for her manner changed. She assumed a spurious dignity and sat down, arranging her short black skirts about her thin legs with great care.

"I've come to consult you, Mr. Campion," she said. "I'm putting all my cards on the table. I want to know if you're satisfied about that funeral?"

"It wasn't much to do with me," I countered, temporarily taken aback.

"Oh, wasn't it? Well, why was you there? That's pinked you, hasn't it? I'm a straightforward girl, Mr. Campion, and I want a straight answer. There was something funny about that funeral, and you know it."

"Look here," I said, "I'm perfectly willing to help you. Suppose you tell me why you think I can."

She looked at me steadily. "You've been to a good school, haven't you?" she said. "I always think it helps a man to have gone to a good school. Then you know he's a gentleman; I always say that. Well, I'll trust you. I don't often. And if you let me down, well, I've been silly again, that's all. I was engaged to marry Roly Peters, Mr. Campion, and then he went and died in a hole-and-corner nursing home and left all his money to his brother. If you don't think that's suspicious, I do."

I hesitated. "You think it's odd because he left his brother everything?" I began.

Effie Rowlandson interrupted me.

"I think it's funny he died at all, if you ask me," she said. "I'd threatened him with a lawyer, I had really. I had the letters and everything."

I said nothing, and she grew very pink.

"Think what you like about me, Mr. Campion," she said, "but I've got feelings and I've worked very hard to get married. I think he's done the dirty on me. If he's hiding I'll find him, if it's the last thing I do."

She sat looking at me like a suddenly militant sparrow.

"I came to you," she said, "because I heard you were a detective and I liked your face."

"Splendid! But why come here?" I demanded. "Why come to Kepesake, of all places?"

Effie Rowlandson drew a deep breath. "I'll tell you the truth, Mr. Campion," she said.

Once again her lashes flickered, and I felt that our brief period of plain dealing was at an end.

"I've got a friend in this village, and he's seen my photographs of Roly Peters. He's an old man, known me for years."

She paused, and eyed me to see if I was with her or against her, and apparently she was reassured, for she went on breathlessly:

"A few days ago he wrote me, this friend of mine did. 'There's a gentleman in the village very like a friend of yours,' he wrote. 'If I were you I'd come and have a look at him. It might be worth your while.' I came as soon as I could, and when I got here I found this man I'd come to see had got himself killed only this morning. I heard you were in the village, so I came along."

I began to follow her. "You want to identify him?" I said.

She nodded resolutely.

"Why come to me? Why not go to the authorities?"

Her reply was disarming. "Well, you see, I felt I knew you," she said.

I considered. The advantages of a witness at this juncture were inestimable.

"When can you be down at the police station?"

"I'd like to go now."

It was late for the country, and I said so, but she was adamant.

"I've made up my mind to it and I shan't sleep if I've got it hanging over me till tomorrow. Take me down now in your car. Go on, you know you can. I am being a nuisance, aren't I? But I'm like that. If I make up my mind to a thing, I fret till I've done it. I should be quite ill by the morning, I should really."

There was nothing else for it. I knew from experience that it is safest to catch a witness as soon as he appears on the scene.

I rang the bell, and told the girl who answered it to send Lugg round with the car. Then, leaving Miss Rowlandson in the breakfast-room, I went to find Janet.

It was not a very pleasant interview. Janet is a dear girl, but she can be most obtuse. When she went to bed, which she did with some dignity a few minutes after I had located her, I went back to the breakfast-room.

Lugg seemed a little surprised when I appeared with Miss Rowlandson. I tucked her into the back of the car, and climbed into the front seat beside him. He let in the clutch, and as we roared down the drive in fourth he leant towards me.

"Ever see a cat come out of a dawg-kennel?" he murmured, and added when I stared at him: "Gives you a bit of a turn. That's all."

We drove on in silence. I began to feel that my friend, Miss Effie Rowlandson, was going to be a responsibility.

It was a strange night with a great moon sailing in an infinite sky. Small odd-shaped banks of cumulus clouds swam over it from time to time, but for the most part it remained bland and bald as the knob on a brass bedstead.

Kepesake, which is a frankly picturesque village by day, was mysterious in the false light. The high trees were deep and shadowy and hid the small houses, while the square tower of the church looked squat and menacing against the transparent sky. It was a secret village through which we sped on what I for one felt was our rather ghastly errand.

When we pulled up outside the cottage which is also the Police Station, there was only a single light in an upstairs room, and I leant over the back of my seat.

"Are you sure you wouldn't rather leave it until the morning?" I ventured.

She answered me through clenched teeth. "No, thank you, Mr. Campion. I've made up my mind to go through with it. I've got to know."

I left them in the car and went down the path to rouse someone. Pussey himself came out almost at once, and was wonderfully obliging considering he had been on the point of going to bed. We conferred in whispers out of deference to the darkness.

"That's all right, sir," he said in reply to my apologies. "Us wants a bit o' help in this business, and that's the truth now, so it is. If the lady can tell us anything about the deceased it's more than the landlord of his flat in London can. We'll go round the side, sir, if you don't mind."

I fetched the others, and together we formed a grim little procession on the gravel path leading round to the yard behind the cottage. Pussey unlocked the gates, and we crossed the tidy little square to the slate-roofed shed which looked like a small village schoolroom, and was not.

I took Effie Rowlandson's arm. She was shivering and her teeth were chattering, but she was not a figure of negligible courage.

Pussey was tact itself. "There's a light switch just inside the door," he said. "Now, Miss there ain't nothin' to shock you. Just a moment, sir; I'll go first."

He unlocked the door, and we stood huddled together on the stone step. Pussey turned over the light switch.

"Now," he said, and a moment later swallowed with a sound in which incredulity was mixed with dismay. The room remained as I had seen it that afternoon, save for one startling innovation. The table in the middle of the floor was dismantled. The cotton sheet lay upon the ground, spread out as though a careless riser had flung it aside.

Pig Peters had gone.

CHAPTER 8

The Wheels Go Round

THERE WAS A LONG uncomfortable pause. A moment before I had seen Pig's outline under the cotton clearly in my mind's eye. Now the image was dispelled so ruthlessly that I felt mentally stranded. The room was very cold and quiet. Lugg stepped ponderously forward.

"Lost the perishin' corpse now?" he demanded, and he spoke so truculently that I knew he was rattled. "Lumme, Inspector, I 'ope your 'elmet's under lock and key."

Pussey stood looking down at the dismantled table, and his pleasant yokel face was pale.

"That's a wonderful funny thing," he began, and looked round the ill-lit barren little room as though he expected to find an explanation for the mystery on its blank walls.

It was a moment of alarm, the night so silent, the place so empty and the bedraggled cotton pall on the ground.

Pussey would have spoken again had it not been for Effie Rowlandson's exhibition. Her nerve deserted her utterly and she drew away from me, her head strained back as she began to scream, her mouth twisted into an O of terror. It was nerve-racking, and I seized her by the shoulders and shook her so violently that her teeth rattled.

It silenced her, of course. Her final shriek was cut off in the middle, and she looked up at me angrily.

"Stop it!" I said. "Do you want to rouse the village?"

She put her hands to push me away.

"I'm frightened," she said. "I don't know what I'm doing. What's happened to him? You told me he was here. I was going to look at him, and now he's gone."

She began to cry noisily. Pussey glanced at her and then at me.

"Perhaps that'd be best if the young lady went home," he suggested reasonably.

Miss Rowlandson clung to me. "Don't leave me," she said. "I'm not going down to 'The Feathers' in the dark. I won't, I tell you, I won't! Not while he's about, alive."

"It's all right," I began soothingly. "Lugg'll drive you down. There's nothing to be alarmed about. There's been a mistake. The body's been moved. Perhaps the undertaker—"

Pussey raised his head as he heard the last word.

"No," he said. "That was in here an hour ago, because I looked."

Effie began to cry again. "I won't go with him," she said. "I won't go with anyone but you. I'm frightened. You got me into this. You must get me out of it. Take me home! Take me home!"

She made an astounding amount of noise, and Pussey looked at me beseechingly.

"Perhaps if you would drive the young lady down, sir," he suggested diffidently, "that would ease matters up here, in a manner of speaking. I better get on the telephone to Sir Leo right away."

I glanced at Lugg appealingly, but he avoided my eyes, and Miss Rowlandson laid her head on my shoulder in an ecstasy of tears.

The situation had all the unreality and acute discomfort of a nightmare. Outside the shed the yard was ghostly in the false light. It was hot, and there was not a breath of wind anywhere. Effie was trembling so violently that I thought she might collapse.

"I'll be back in a minute," I said to Pussey, and hurried her down the gravel path to the waiting car.

"The Feathers Inn" is at the far end of the village. It stands by itself at the top of a hill, and is reputed to have the best beer, if not the best accommodation, in the neighborhood.

Effie Rowlandson scrambled into the front seat, and when I climbed in beside her she drew close to me, still weeping.

"I've had a shock," she snivelled. "I'd prepared myself and then it wasn't necessary. That was one thing. Then I realized Roly got out by himself. You didn't know Roly Peters as well as I did, Mr. Campion. When I heard he'd been killed I didn't really believe it. He was clever, and he was cruel. He's about somewhere, hiding."

"He was dead this afternoon," I said brutally. "Very dead. And since miracles don't happen nowadays he's probably dead still. There's nothing to get so excited about. I'm sorry you should have had a rotten experience, but there's probably some very ordinary explanation for the disappearance of the body."

I was rather shocked to hear myself talking so querulously. There had been something very disturbing in the incident. The elusiveness of Pig dead was becoming illogical and alarming.

As we came out of the village on to the strip of heath which lay silent and deserted in the cold secretive light, she shuddered.

"I'm not an imaginative girl, Mr. Campion," she said, "but you read of funny things happening, don't you? Suppose he was to rise up behind one of these banks of stones by the side of the road and come out towards us..."

"Shut up," I said, even more violently than I had intended. "You'll frighten yourself into a fit, my child. I assure you there's some perfectly reasonable explanation for all this. When you get into 'The Feathers' make them give you a hot drink and go to bed. You'll find the mystery's been cleared up by the morning."

She drew away from me. "Oh, you're hard," she said with a return of her old manner. "I said you were hard. I like hard people, I do really."

Her lightning changes of mood disconcerted me, and I was glad when we pulled up outside the pub. The fine old lath and plaster front was in darkness, which was not astonishing, for it was nearly midnight.

"Which door is it?" I inquired.

"The one marked Club Room. I expect it'll be locked."

I left her in the car while I tapped on the door she indicated. For a time there was no response, and I was getting restive at the delay when I heard a furtive movement on the inside. I tapped again, and this time the door was opened.

"I say, you're fearfully late," said the last voice I expected, and Gilbert Whippet of all people thrust a pale face out into the moonlight.

I gaped at him, and he had the grace to seem vaguely disturbed to see me.

"Oh...er...Campion," he said. "Hello! Terribly late, isn't it?"

He was backing into the dark pit of the doorway when I pulled myself together.

"Hey," I said, catching him by the sleeve. "Here, Whippet, where are you going?"

He did not resist me, but made no attempt to come out into the light. Moreover, I felt that once I let him go he would fade quietly into the background.

"I was going to bed," he murmured, no doubt in reply to my question. "I heard you knock, so I opened the door."

"You stay and talk to me," I commanded. "What are you doing here, anyway?"

In spite of myself I heard the old censorious note creeping into my tone. Whippet is so very vague that he forces one into an unusual directness.

He did not answer me, and I repeated the question.

"Here?" he said, looking up at the pub. "Oh yes, I'm staying here. Only for a day or two."

He was infuriating, and I quite forgot the girl until I heard her step behind me.

"Mr. Whippet," she began breathlessly, "he's gone! The body's gone! What shall we do?"

Whippet turned his pale eyes towards her, and I thought I detected a warning in the glance.

"Ah, Miss Rowlandson," he said. "You've been out? You're late, aren't you?"

I was glad to see she wasn't playing, either.

"The body's gone," she repeated. "Roly Peters's body is gone."

The information seemed to sink in. For a moment he looked positively intelligent.

"Lost it?" he said. "Oh!... Awkward. Holds things up so."

His voice trailed away into silence, and he suddenly shook hands with me.

"Glad to have seen you, Campion. I'll look you up some time. Er—good night."

He stepped back into the doorway, and Effie followed him. With great presence of mind I put my foot in the jamb.

"Look here, Whippet," I said, "if you can do anything to help us in this matter, or if you know anything, you'd better come out with it. What do you know about Peters, anyway?"

He blinked at me.

"Oh…nothing. I'm just staying here. I've heard the talk, of course…"

I caught his sleeve again just as he was disappearing.

"You had one of those letters," I said. "Have you had any more?"

"About the mole? Yes. Yes, as a matter of fact, I have, Campion. I've got it somewhere. I showed it to Miss Rowlandson. I say, it's terribly awkward you losing the body. Have you looked in the river?"

It was such an unexpected question that it irritated me unreasonably.

"Why on earth in the river?" I said. "D'you know anything?"

In my excitement I must have held him a little more tightly than I had intended, for he suddenly shook himself free.

"I should look in the river," he said. "I mean, it's so obvious, isn't it?"

He stepped back and closed the door with himself and Miss Rowlandson inside. I still had my foot there, however, and he opened it again. He seemed embarrassed.

"It's fearfully late," he said. "I don't mean to be rude, Campion. I'll look you up tomorrow, if I may, but there's no point in your doing anything at all until you've found the body, is there?"

I hesitated. There was a great deal in what Whippet said. I was itching to get back, and yet there was evidently much he could explain. What on earth was he doing there with Effie Rowlandson, for one thing?

In that moment of hesitation I was lost. He moved forward, and as I stepped backward involuntarily the door was gently, almost politely, closed in my face.

I cursed him, but decided he could wait. I hurried back to the car and turned her. As I raced down to the Police Station I tried to reconcile Whippet's reappearance with the whole mysterious business.

I covered the half mile in something under a minute, and pulled up outside Pussey's cottage at the same moment that another car arrived from the opposite direction. As I climbed out I recognized Leo's respectable Humber. Pepper Junior was driving, and Leo hailed me from the tonneau.

"Is that you, Campion? Most extraordinary business! Pussey told me over the phone."

I went up to the car and opened the door.

"Are you coming, sir?" I said.

"Yes, my boy, yes. Should have been here before, but I stopped to pick up Bathwick here. Seems to have had a little accident on the way home from our place tonight."

He put up his hand and turned on the light as he spoke, and I stared down into the pale, embarrassed face of the Reverend Smedley Philip Bathwick, who smiled at me with uncharacteristic friendliness. He was wringing wet. His dinner jacket clung to him, and his dog-collar was a sodden rag.

"Been in the river, he tells me," said Leo.

CHAPTER 9

"And a Very Good Day to You, Sir"

"THE RIVER?" I echoed, Whippet's idiotic remark returning to me. "Really?"

Bathwick giggled. It was a purely nervous sound, but Leo scowled at him.

"Well, hardly," he said. "I was taking a short cut home across the saltings and I stumbled into one of the dykes. I'd come out without my torch. I made my way back to the road, and Sir Leo very kindly picked me up and gave me a lift."

It was a fantastic story in view of the moonlight, which was so bright that colours were almost distinguishable, and I thought Leo must notice it. He had a one-track mind, however. His one desire was to get back to the scene of the disappearance.

"Never mind, never mind. Soon get you home now," he

said. "Pepper'll take you along. Make yourself a hot toddy. Wrap yourself in a blanket and you'll come to no harm."

"Er—thank you, thank you very much," said Bathwick. "I should like nothing better. I feel I must express—"

We heard no more, for Pepper Junior, who doubtless shared his employer's anxiety to get to the scene of the excitement in the shortest possible time, let in the clutch and Bathwick was whisked away.

I was sorry to lose him. His astonishing friendliness towards me was not the least fishy circumstance of his brief appearance.

"Where did you find him?" I asked Leo.

"On the lower road. Nearly ran him down. He's all right just—a duckin'." Leo was fighting with the catch of the police-station gate as he spoke and appeared profoundly uninterested.

"Yes, I know," I said. "But he left Highwaters at about a quarter to ten. I thought Kingston was going to run him home?"

"So he did, so he did," said Leo, sighing with relief as we got the wicket open. "Kingston put him down at the White Barn corner, and he said he'd strike his way home across the marshes. Can't be more than five hundred yards. But the silly feller stumbled into a dyke, lost his nerve, and made his way back to the road. Perfectly simple, Campion. No mystery there. Come on, my boy, come on. We're wastin' time."

"But it's now midnight," I objected. "It couldn't have taken him a couple of hours to scramble out of a dyke."

"Might have done," said Leo irritably. "Backboneless feller. Anyway, we can't bother about him now. Got somethin' serious to think about. I don't like monkey-business with a corpse. It's not a bit like my district. It's indecent. I tell you

I feel it, Campion. Ah, here's Pussey. Anythin' to report, my man?"

Pussey and Lugg came up together. I could see their faces quite plainly, and I wondered how Bathwick could possibly have avoided seeing a rabbit-hole, much less a dyke.

Pussey, I saw at once, was well over his first superstitious alarm. At the moment he was less mystified than shocked.

"That's a proper nasty thing, sir," he said, "so that is, now."

He led us into the shed and, with Lugg remaining mercifully silent in the background, gave us a fairly concise account of his investigations.

"All these windows were bolted on the inside, sir, the same as you see them now, and the door was locked. At a quarter to eleven I went round the station just to see everything was all right for the night, and the body was here then. After that I went in to the front of the house, and I stayed there for some little time until I went up to my bedroom. I was just thinking about bed when Mr. Campion here arrived with the young lady and Mr. Lugg, and we come round here and made the discovery, sir."

He paused, took a deep breath, and Leo spluttered.

"Did the key leave your possession?"

"No, sir."

Leo's natural reaction to the story of a miracle is to take it as read that someone is lying. I could hear him boiling quietly at my side.

"Pussey, I've always found you a very efficient officer," he began with dangerous calm, "but you're askin' me to believe in a fairy story. If the body didn't go through the windows it must have gone through the door, and if you had the only key—"

Pussey coughed. "Excuse me, sir," he began, "but Mr. Lugg and me we made a kind of discovery, like. This building was put up by Mr. Henry Royle, the builder in the Street, and Mr. Lugg and me we noticed that several other buildings in this yard, sir, which were put up at the same time, all have the same locks, like."

Leo's rage subsided and he became interested.

"Any of the other keys here missin'?"

"No, sir; but as Mr. Royle has done a lot of work hereabouts lately, it doesn't seem unlikely—?"

He broke off on the question.

Leo swore, and it seemed to relieve him.

"Oh, well, we shan't get any help there," he rumbled. "Wonder you trouble to lock the place at all, Pussey. Damned inefficient. Typical of the whole county," he added to me under his breath.

But Pussey had more to offer. With considerable pride he led us over the rough grass by the side of the shed to the tarred fence which marked the boundary line of police property. Three boards had been kicked down and there was a clear way into the narrow lane beyond.

"That's new," he said. "That's been done tonight."

A cursory search of the lane revealed nothing. The ground was hard and the surface was baked mud interspersed with tufts of grass. It was Pussey who put the general thought into words.

"Whoever moved him must'a done it between quarter to eleven and twenty-five minutes past. Seems very likely that was done with a car, or a cart. He was a heavy fellow. If you'll excuse me, sir, I think the best thing is for us to wait till the morning and then question all those as live nearby. Seems like we can't do nothing while that's dark."

In the end we left it at that. Pepper Junior collected Leo and I sent Lugg back with the Lagonda. Pussey went to bed and I walked off down the grassy lane behind the shed. The moon was sinking and already there were faint streaks of light in the east. It was colder and I was in the mood to walk home.

The lane went on for some distance between high hedges. Pussey had given me clear directions how to get on to the road again, and I sauntered on, my mind on the business.

Leo and Pussey, I saw, were outraged. The murder had shaken them up, but this apparently wanton disturbance of the dead shocked them both deeply.

As I thought of it, it seemed to me that this element was perhaps the most enlightening thing I had noticed so far, because, although I knew I had no proof of it, it seemed to me that it constituted a complete let-out for Leo's particular band of friends who had gathered round Poppy in her trouble. Whereas any one of them might quite easily have staged the slightly ludicrous accident which had killed Pig, I could not see any of them dragging his body about afterwards in this extraordinary pointless fashion.

I was considering those who were left, and Bathwick was figuring largely in my mind, when I turned out of the lane on to a grass field which rose up to form a considerable hill, circular against the skyline. I knew I had to skirt this field and pass through another before I came to the road, if I was to avoid an unnecessary couple of miles.

It was almost dark at the bottom of the hill, and as I plodded on, lost in my thoughts, there came to me suddenly over the brow of the hill a sound at once so human and so terrifying that I felt the hair on my scalp rising.

It was Pig's cough.

The night was very still, and I heard the rattle in the larynx, the whoop, and even the puff at the end of it.

For a moment I stood still, a prey to all the ridiculous fears of childhood. Then I set off up the hill at a double. The wind whistled in my ears and my heart was thumping.

Suddenly, as I reached the brow, I saw something silhouetted against the grey sky. This was so unexpected that I paused to gape at it. It was a tripod with something else which I at first took to be a small machine-gun, and which turned out to be an old-fashioned telescope mounted upon it.

I approached this cautiously, and had almost reached it when a figure rose up out of the earth beside it and stood waiting for me. He was against what light there was and I could only see his small silhouette. I stopped, and for want of something better, said what must have been the silliest thing in the world in the circumstances. I said "Good-day."

"And a very good day to you, sir," answered one of the most unpleasant voices I have ever heard in all my life.

He came towards me and I recognized him with relief by his peculiar mincing walk.

"Perhaps I have the advantage of you, sir," he began. "You are Mr. Campion?"

"Yes," I said. "And you're Mr. Hayhoe."

He laughed, a little affected sound.

"It will serve," he murmured. "It will serve. I was looking forward to an interview with you today, sir. I was wondering how I could manage it with a certain amount of privacy. This is a most unexpected pleasure. I didn't expect to find a man of your age wandering about in the dawn. Most young men nowadays prefer to spend the best part of their day in their beds."

"You're up early yourself," I said, glancing at the telescope. "Waiting to see the sunrise?"

"Yes," he said, and laughed again. "That and other things."

It was a mad conversation up there on the hill at two o'clock in the morning, and it went through my mind that he must be one of those fashionable nature-lovers who rush round the country identifying birds. He soon disabused me of that idea, however.

"I take it you are making investigations concerning the death of that unfortunate fellow Harris?" he said. "Now, Mr. Campion, I can be very useful to you. I wish to make you a proposition. For a reasonable sum, the amount to be settled between us, I will undertake to give you certain very interesting information, information which it would take you a very long time to collect alone and which should lead you to a very successful conclusion of the case. Your professional reputation will be enhanced, and I shall, of course, take none of the kudos. Now, suppose we come to terms…"

I am afraid I laughed at him. This is the kind of offer which I have had so often. I thought of the cough I had heard.

"Harris was a relation of yours, I suppose?" I observed.

He stiffened a little and shrugged his shoulders.

"A nephew," he said, "and not a very dutiful one. He was quite a wealthy young man, you see, and I—well as you can imagine, I am not the sort of man who normally spends his holidays in a wretched workman's hovel or his evenings traipsing about the barren countryside."

He was rather a terrible old man, but I was glad I had cleared up the mystery of the cough.

It was then that I remembered something. After all, so far, I myself was the only person to connect Roly Peters with Oswald Harris, with the possible exception of Effie Rowlandson, who merely had her suspicions.

"Let me see," I murmured, "that was your nephew Rowland Peters, wasn't it?"

To my intense regret he brushed the inference aside.

"I have several nephews, Mr. Campion, or, rather, I had," he said with spurious dignity. "I hate to press the point, but I regard this as a business interview. Terms first, if you please. Shall we say five hundred guineas for a complete and private explanation of the whole business? Or, of course, I might split up the lots, as it were."

While he was rambling on I was thinking, and at this point I had an inspiration.

"Mr. Hayhoe," I said, "what about the mole?"

A little shrill sound escaped him, but he bit it off instantly.

"Oh!" he said, and there was cautiousness and respect in his voice, "you know about the mole, do you?"

CHAPTER 10

The Parson's Dram

I DID NOT REPLY. In the circumstances of my extreme ignorance there was very little I could say. I remained silent, therefore, and, I hope, enigmatic. However, he was not to be drawn.

"I hadn't thought of the creature myself," he said unexpectedly, "but there may be something there. It's a valuable contribution. You seem to be unexpectedly intelligent, if I may say so without offence."

He sighed and sat down on the grass.

"Yes," he continued, clasping his knees. "Thinking it over we ought to go far, you and I, once we can come to an understanding. Now, about this question of terms…I hate to insist upon the subject, but at the moment my financial affairs are in considerable disorder. How far would you be prepared to meet me?"

"Not to a pound," I said flatly, but with politeness. "If

you know anything about the death of your nephew it's your obvious duty to go to the police with it."

Mr. Hayhoe shrugged his shoulders. "Oh, well," he said regretfully, "I gave you the opportunity. You can't deny that."

I turned away expecting him to call me back, which he did.

"My dear young man," he protested when I had taken a few steps down the hill, "don't be precipitate. Let us talk this thing over reasonably. I have certain information which is of value to you. Why should we quarrel?"

"If you knew anything of importance," I said over my shoulder, "you'd hardly dare to talk about it."

"Ah, you don't understand." He seemed greatly relieved. "My own situation is perfectly safe. I have nothing to lose, everything to gain. My position is simple. I happen to possess an asset which I intend to realize. There are two likely purchasers: one is yourself, and the other is a certain person I need not name. Naturally, I shall dispose to the highest bidder."

I was growing weary of him. "Mr. Hayhoe," I said, "I am tired. I want to go to bed. You are wasting my time. You are also making a fool of yourself. I'm sorry to be so explicit, but there it is."

He got up. "Look here, Campion," he said with a complete change of tone, his artificiality dropping from him and a wheedling note taking its place, "I could tell you something interesting if I wanted to. The police can pull me in and bully rag me, but they can't hold me because they've nothing on me. I shan't talk to them and they can't make me. I can put you on to the right track for a consideration. What's it worth to you?"

"At this stage, very little," I said. "Half a crown, perhaps."

He laughed. "I think I can get more than that," he said softly. "Very much more. However, I'm not a rich man. Between ourselves, at the moment I'm very short indeed. Suppose we meet tomorrow morning, not quite as early as this? Say, seven o'clock. That gives me a clear twenty-four hours. If I can't get satisfaction in other quarters, well, I may bate my price a little. What do you say?"

He was an unpleasant piece of work, but I liked him better in this mood.

"We might have a chat about the mole," I conceded ungraciously.

He cocked an eye at me. "Very well," he agreed. "About the mole and—other things. I'll meet you here, then, at seven o'clock tomorrow morning—"

As I turned away an idea occurred to me.

"About your other purchaser," I said. "I shouldn't approach Sir Leo if I were you."

This time his laugh was spontaneous.

"You're not quite so clever as I thought you were," he said, and I went off down the hill with something to think about. Quite frankly, until that moment I had not seen him as a possible blackmailer.

At the time I thought I was justified in letting him cook for twenty-four hours, but at that time, as I have said, I did not know the type of person we were up against. Whenever I am apt to get over-pleased with myself, I remember that little chat on the hill-side.

As I came wearily up the drive at Highwaters it was full dawn. The air was magnificent, the sky a translucent blue, and the birds were roaring at one another in undisturbed abandonment.

I suspected the french windows in the dining-room had been left unlatched, and as I went round to them a rather unfortunate thing happened. Janet, who had no business to be awake at such an hour, came out on her balcony and caught me. I looked up to see her staring down at my slinking dinner-jacketed figure with mingled surprise and contempt.

"Good morning," I said innocently.

Two bright spots of colour appeared on her cheeks.

"I hope you saw Miss Rowlandson home safely," she said, and went back to her room before I could explain.

I had a tepid bath and slept for a couple of hours, but I was waiting for Leo when he appeared round about eight o'clock. We went for a stroll round the garden before breakfast, and I put my request to him.

"Have the feller watched?" he said. "Good idea. I'll phone down to Pussey. Extraordinary name, Heigh-ho. Must be fictitious. Any reason above general suspicion?"

I told him about the conversation on the hill-top, and at first he wanted to have the man pulled in immediately.

"I don't think I would, sir," I objected. "I don't see how he can be involved himself, unless he's playing an incredibly dangerous game. Leave him loose, and he'll lead us to someone more interesting."

"As you like," he said, "As you like. Prefer the straightforward method myself."

As it happened, of course, he was perfectly right, but none of us knew that then.

Janet did not appear to breakfast, but I had no time to think about her, for Kingston arrived before the meal was over. He was bubbling with excitement, and looked very young for his forty years as he came striding in, his coarse fair hair dishevelled and his rather lazy eyes unwontedly bright.

"I've found it," he announced, before he was well in the room. "I've been up half the night turning over papers, but I tracked it down in the end. The firm I dealt with in Peters's affairs was Skinn, Sutain, and Skinn, of Lincoln's Inn Fields. Any good?"

I took the name down, and he looked at me expectantly.

"I could take the day off and go up and see them for you, if you like," he said. "Or perhaps you'll go yourself?"

I didn't like to damp his enthusiasm, though it occurred to me that his life must be incredibly dull, since he was so anxious to play the detective.

"Well, no," I said. "I think it'll have to wait for the time being. The body's disappeared, you see."

"Really? I say!" He seemed delighted, and chattered on when I explained. "Things are moving, aren't they? I suppose you'll have to leave the solicitors for a day or two. Anything I can do? I've got to run down to Halt Knights to see my young patient, and there are one or two other people I ought to see, but after that I can be at your service entirely."

"I've got to go down to Poppy's," I said. "I'll come with you, if I may."

Leo had left us and was on the telephone in the gun-room, talking to Pussey, when I disturbed him a minute or so later. He listened to my rather hurried story with unexpected intelligence.

"Wait a minute," he said, when I had finished. "You think there may be some connexion between this feller Peters you knew and Harris, and you want me to get the London people to interview these solicitors with a view to their identifying the body. That right?"

"Yes," I said. "There may not be anything in it, but they might make general inquiries there about the two men, Peters and Harris. What I particularly want to know is where Harris got his money—if he was insured or anything. It's rather a shot in the dark, I know, but there's just a chance these people may be useful. I think they'll have to be handled delicately. I mean, I don't think it could be done by phone."

He nodded. "All right, my boy. Anything that helps us to get any nearer to this terrible thing, don't you know...Pussey's going to put a man on to that feller, Heigh-ho."

He paused abruptly, and stood looking at me.

"Let's hope he doesn't lead us to anyone..."

He broke off helplessly.

"I'm coming down to Halt Knights now," I murmured.

He coughed. "I'll follow you down. Don't alarm her, my boy; don't alarm her. Can't bring myself to believe that she's anything to do with it, poor little woman."

Kingston was waiting for me in the drive. He was exuberant. The turn affairs were taking seemed to stimulate him.

"I suppose it's all in the day's work for you?" he said a little enviously, as I climbed in beside him. "But nothing ever happens down here, and I should be inhuman if I wasn't interested. It's rather shocking how the human mind reacts to someone else's tragedy, isn't it? I didn't know Harris, of course, but what I did see of him didn't attract me. I should say the world's a better place without him. I saw him just before he died, you know, or at least an hour or so before, and I remember thinking at the time that he constituted a waste of space."

I was busy with my own problems, but I did not wish to be impolite.

"When was this?" I said absently.

He was anxious to tell me.

"On the stairs at Halt Knights. I was going up to see my

little patient with jaundice, and he came staggering down. I never saw a fellow with such a hangover. He brushed past me, his eyes glazed and his tongue hanging out. Didn't say good morning or anything—you know the type."

"That patient of yours," I said. "She must have been upstairs all through the incident…?"

He turned to me in surprise. "Flossie?" he said. "Yes, she was; but you're on the wrong tack, there. She's away at the back of the house in a little top attic. Besides, you must have a look at her. The poor little beast is a bit better now, but a couple of days ago she couldn't stand, poor kid. However, she may have heard something. I'll ask her."

I told him not to bother, and he went on chattering happily, making all sorts of useless suggestions. When I listened to him at all, he had my sympathy. A life that needs a murder to make it interesting must, I thought, be very slow indeed.

When we arrived he went straight up to see his patient, but I sought out Poppy in the lounge. It was early, and we were alone. She seemed delighted to see me and, as usual, insisted on getting me a drink at once. I followed her into the bar while she mixed it, and hurried to put the question that was on my mind before Kingston should return.

"You say you remember yesterday morning very clearly?" I said. "Did you have a visitor who left here some little time before the accident? Someone who wasn't in the house at the time, but who wandered off within half an hour or so of the trouble?"

She paused in the act of scooping little blocks of ice out of the refrigerator tray.

"No, there was no one," she said, "unless you count the parson."

I took off my spectacles. "Bathwick?"

"Yes. He always comes in round about twelve o'clock. He likes his highballs American fashion, like this thing I'm mixing for you. He never has more than one. Drops in about twelve o'clock, drinks it, and trots out again. I saw him to the door myself yesterday morning. He goes off through the kitchen garden to the stile leading into the Vicarage meadow. Why?"

I stood looking down at the glass in my hand, twirling the ice round and round in the amber liquid, and it was then that I had the whole case under my nose.

Unfortunately, I only saw half of it.

CHAPTER 11

"Why Drown Him?"

I WAS STILL WORKING it out when Poppy laid her hand upon my arm. I turned to find her plump face flushed and anxious.

"Albert," she murmured confidentially, "I can't talk now because Kingston's just coming down, but there's something I want to say to you. Ssh! There he is."

She turned back to the bar and began to bustle among the glasses. Kingston came in, cheerfully superior.

"She's all right now," he said, grinning at Poppy, "or will be in a day or two. Don't let her eat too much grease. Like to come up and see her, Campion?"

Poppy raised her eyebrows at him, and he explained. She began to laugh at us.

"The child hasn't the strength, and she hasn't the wits," she said. "And if she had she wouldn't do it. She's a good little girl, our Flossie. Flossie, indeed! I've never heard of anything so futile."

Kingston was very insistent, however, and his anxiety to keep in the picture might easily have been exasperating if there had been anything pressing to be done. As it was, I went upstairs with him through a maze of corridors and unexpected staircases until we found the little attic under the roof at the far end of the house from the box-room.

As soon as I met Flossie I saw they were right. Her little yellow face was pathetic and disinterested. Kingston asked her questions—Had she heard anything? Had she been out of the room? Had anything unusual happened on the day before?—and she answered "No, sir" to them all with the weary patience of the really ill.

We left her and went along to have another look at the box-room. It was just as I had left it. Kingston was tremendously knowing and important. Evidently he fancied himself in his new role.

"There's a scratch there," he said, pointing to the one I had already noticed. "Does that tell you anything, Campion? It looks fairly new, doesn't it? How about getting some finger-prints?"

I looked at the rough cast sadly, and led him away.

We got rid of him at last. He offered to drive me down to the Police Station, but I refused, explaining that Leo was coming to pick me up. I caught sight of Poppy as I spoke, and saw her turn colour.

We stood in the window together and watched Kingston's car disappear down the drive. She sighed.

"They're *bored*," she said. "They're all bored, poor darlings. He's a nice boy, he doesn't want to be a ghoul; but it'll all give him something to talk about when he goes to see his patients.

It must be terrible going to see people every day if you haven't got anything to tell them, don't you think?"

"Yes," I said dubiously. "I suppose it is. What have you got to tell *me*, by the way?"

She did not answer me immediately, but the colour came into her face, and she looked like some large guilty baby faced with confession.

"I had a few words with Leo yesterday," she began at last. "Not that I mind, of course, although it does do to keep in with one's clients, and—er—friends. I can see that I've annoyed him. I told him a silly lie, and then I didn't like to explain. You can see that happening, can't you?"

She paused and eyed me.

"I can," I said cheerfully.

"The stupid thing is that it doesn't matter," she went on, playing with her rings. "People down here are terrible snobs, Albert."

I didn't quite follow her, and I said so.

"Oh well, it's Hayhoe," she said explosively. "An awful little bounder, Albert, but probably quite human, and he's got to live, like anybody else, hasn't he?"

"Wait a minute," I said. "I've got to get this straight. Is Hayhoe a friend of yours?"

"Oh no, not a *friend*." She brushed the term away irritably. "But he came to me for help last week. "

I was inspired.

"Did he borrow money?"

"Oh no!" She was shocked. "He was very hard up, poor man. He told me his story, and I may have lent him a pound or two. But you wouldn't say he'd borrowed money. You see, Ducky, it was like this—he came to me about two days after that wretched man Harris settled here. I was just beginning to find out the sort of man Harris was when this poor old chap came along, asked to see me privately, and told me the whole thing. Harris was his nephew, you see, and there'd been a lot of jiggery-pokery going on, and somehow—I forget quite how—this little tick Harris had done the old man out of all his money. He wanted to see him on the quiet to get it back, and he wanted me to help him. I let him into Harris's room—"

"You what!" I said aghast.

"Well, I showed him where it was, and let him go upstairs. That was some days ago. There was an awful row, and poor little Hayhoe came running out with a flea in his ear, since when he's never been near the place—until last night, when Leo happened to see him. I didn't want to explain the whole story—because there's no point in that man getting into a row when he wasn't even near the house yesterday morning—and so I was short with Leo, and he is cross. Put it all straight for me, Albert. Have another drink."

I refused the one and promised to my best with the other.

"How do you know Hayhoe wasn't about yesterday morning?" I said.

She looked at me as though I was an imbecile.

"Well, I know what goes on in my own house, I hope," she said. "I know it's the fashion round here to think I'm a dear silly old fool, but I'm not completely demented. Besides, everybody's been questioned. That doesn't come into it."

"Why did Hayhoe come down here yesterday?"

"In the evening? Well"—she was hesitant again—"it's difficult to explain. He came to tell me that he knew how I felt being surrounded by snobby county people in a trouble like this, and he offered his help as a man of the world."

She was thoughtful for a moment or two.

"I really think he came to get a drink, if you ask me," she added with that touch of the practical which always redeems her.

"Did you lend him any more money?" I murmured diffidently.

"Only half a crown," she said. "Don't tell Leo. He thinks I'm such a fool."

My mind went back to Bathwick, and in the end she took me out and showed me the little path through the kitchen garden which led down to the Vicarage stile. It was a quiet little path, almost entirely hidden by the foliage of the fruit trees. As we came back, I turned to her.

"Look here," I said, "I know the police have badgered your staff about the events of yesterday morning, and I don't want to rattle them again, but do you think you could find out by unobtrusive, gossipy questioning if there was anybody pottering about the upper storeys some little time before the accident? Bathwick could have come back, you see, quite easily."

"A parson!" said Poppy. "Well…! You don't think…? Oh, Albert, you can't!"

"Of course not," I said hastily. "I only wondered if he could have got upstairs. It'd be interesting, that's all."

"I'll find out," she said with decision.

I thanked her and added a warning note about the law of slander.

"Don't tell *me*," she said, and added, brightening, "Is that the car?"

We hurried down to meet it, Poppy patting her tight grey

curls as she went. But it was Lugg in the Lagonda and not
Leo who pulled up outside the front door. He beckoned to me
mysteriously, and as I hurried up I saw that his great moon of
a face betrayed unusual excitement.

"'Op in," he commanded. "The General wants you down
at the station. Got something there for you."

"Have they found the body?"

He seemed disappointed. "Got your second-sight outfit
workin' again, I see," he said. "Morning, ma'am." He leered at
Poppy over my shoulder as he spoke, out of deference, I felt
sure, to the memory of myriad past beers.

"I'm awfully sorry," I explained to her. "I've got to go. Leo's
waiting for me down at the police station. Something's turned
up. I'll send him along when the excitement's over."

She patted my arm. "Do," she said earnestly. "Do. He's a
pet, Albert. One of the very best. Tell him I've been silly and
I'm sorry, but—but he's not to mention it when he sees me."

I climbed in beside Lugg. "Where was it?" I demanded
as we raced off.

"In the river. Calm as you please. Bloke in a fishin' boat
picked it up. If we 'ad your magic seashell 'ere p'raps that could
tell us somethin'."

I was not listening to him. I was thinking of Whippet. Whippet
and the anonymous letters, Whippet and Effie Rowlandson, and
now Whippet and his extraordinary guess—if it was a guess. I
couldn't imagine where he fitted into the picture. He upset all my
calculations. I decided I must have a chat with him.

Lugg was sulking. "It seems to be a funny place we've come
to," he said. "First they bang a chap on 'is 'ead and then they chuck
'im in the river…some persons aren't never satisfied, reelly."

I sat up. That was the point that had been bothering me

all along. Why the river, where the corpse was almost certain to be found, sooner or later?

By the time we arrived at the little mortuary the obvious had sunk in. Leo was there and Pussey, and with them the two excited fishermen, who had made the discovery. I took Leo on one side, but he would not listen to me immediately. He was bubbling.

"It's an outrage," he said. "It's a disgraceful thing. It shocks me, Campion. In my own village! There was no point in it. Wanton mischief."

"D'you think so?" I said, and I made a certain suggestion.

He stood looking at me and his blue eyes were incredulous. For a policeman, Leo has an amazing faith in the innate decency of his fellow men.

"We want an old man," I said. "Someone with the necessary skill, of course, but someone you can trust to hold his tongue. Anyone locally do?"

He considered. "There's old Professor Farringdon over at Rushberry," he said at last. "He did something of the sort for us some time ago. But you can see for yourself that the cause of death is obvious. Are we justified in having an autopsy?"

"In the case of violent death one's always justified in having an autopsy," I pointed out.

He nodded. "When you saw the body yesterday, did you notice anything then to put such an idea in your head?"

"No," I said truthfully. "No, I didn't. But this makes all the difference. Water has a peculiar property, hasn't it?"

He put his head on one side.

"How d'you mean?"

"Well, it washes things," I said, and I went off to find Whippet.

CHAPTER 12

The Disturbing Element

I HAD ALMOST REACHED the car when I remembered something which had slipped my mind in the excitement of the moment. I hurried back and sought out Pussey.

"Don't you worry, sir. We've put a man on him," he said reassuringly in reply to my question.

I still hesitated. "Hayhoe is slippery," I ventured, "and also it's most important that he's not alarmed."

Pussey was not offended, but he seemed to think that I was a little fussy.

"Young Birkin'll follow him and he won't know it no more than if he was being trailed by a ferret," he said. "You can set your mind at rest."

All this was very comforting, and I was going off again when Leo buttonholed me. He was still dubious about the necessity of an autopsy, and in the end I had to go back and take another look at Pig's pathetic body. There were one or two interesting signs when we looked for them, and in the end I left him convinced.

By this time it was comparatively late, and I arrived at "The Feathers" just before two o'clock. The landlady, a typical East-Anglian, gaunt of body and reticent of speech, was not helpful. It took me some time to get it into her head that it was Whippet I wanted to see.

"Oh," she said at last, "a fair young gentleman, soft-spoken like, almost a natural, as you might say. Well, he's not here."

"But he slept here last night," I persisted.

"Yes, yes, so he did, and that's the truth now," she agreed, "but he's not here now."

"Is he coming back?"

"I couldn't say."

It occurred to me that Whippet must have told her to keep quiet, and this was extremely unlike him. My interest in him grew.

There was no sign of Miss Rowlandson, either. She, too, appeared to have gone out. But whether they went together or separately the landlady was not prepared to tell me.

In the end I had to go back to Highwaters unsatisfied. I was late for lunch, of course, and Pepper served me alone in the dining-room, sorrow and disappointment apparent in every line of his sleek body.   '

What with one thing and another I was falling headlong in his estimation.

When the meal was over he turned to me.

"Miss Janet is in the rose garden, sir," he said, conveying clearly that, murder or no murder, he thought a guest owed a certain deference to his hostess.

I took the rebuke meekly and went out to make amends. It was one of those vivid summer days which are hot without being uncomfortable. The garden was ablaze with flowers and the air serene and peaceful.

As I walked down the grass path between the lavender hedges I heard the sound of voices, and something familiar about one of them caught my attention. Two deck-chairs were placed side by side on the rose lawn with their backs to me, and I heard Janet laugh.

At the sound of my approach her companion rose, and as I saw his head and shoulders appearing over the back of the chair I experienced an odd sensation which was half relief and half an unwarrantable exasperation. It was Whippet himself. Very cool and comfortable he looked, too, in his neat white flannels. His opening words were not endearing.

"Campion! Found you at last," he said. "Er—good. I've been searching for you, my dear fellow, searching all over the place. Here and there."

He moved a languid hand about a foot in either direction.

"I've been busy," I said gracelessly. "Hello, Janet."

She smiled up at me. "This is a nice friend of yours," she said with slightly unnecessary accent on the first word. "Do sit down."

"That's right, do," Whippet agreed. "There's a chair over there," he added, pointing to a pile on the other end of the lawn.

I fetched it, opened it, and sat down opposite them. Whippet watched me put it up with interest.

"Complicated things," he observed.

I waited for him to go on, but he seemed quite content to

lie basking in the sun, with Janet, looking very lovely in white furbelows at his side.

I began boldly. "It's been found, you know—in the river."

He nodded. "So I heard in the village. The whole place is terribly shaken by the tragedy, don't you think? Extraordinary restless spirit pervades the place—have you noticed it?"

He was infuriating, and again I experienced that desire to cuff him which I had felt so strongly on our first adult meeting.

"You've got rather a lot to explain yourself," I said, wishing that Janet would go away.

To my surprise he answered me intelligently.

"I know," he said. "I know. That's why I've been looking for you. There's Miss Rowlandson, for one thing. She's terribly upset. She's gone down to the Vicarage now. I didn't know what to advise."

"The Vicarage?" I echoed. "What on earth for?" Janet, I noticed, was sitting up with interest.

"Oh, help, you know," said Whippet vaguely. "When in doubt in a village one always goes to the parson, doesn't one? Good works and that sort of thing. Oh, yes—and that reminds me, what about this? It came this morning. As soon as I saw it, I thought 'Campion ought to have a look at this; this'll interest Campion.' Have you had one?"

He took a folded sheet of typing-paper out of his wallet as he spoke, and handed it to me.

"The same postmark as the others," he said. "Funny, isn't it? I didn't know anyone knew I was staying at 'The Feathers,' except you, and—well, I mean you'd hardly have the time, would you, even if you—"

His voice trailed away into silence, and I read the third

anonymous letter. This one was very short, typed on the same typewriter and with the same meticulous accuracy:

> "*Although the skinner is at hand his ease is in the earth.*
> "*He waiteth patiently. Peace and hope are in his warm heart.*
> "*He foldeth his hands upon his belly.*
> "*Faith is his that can remove the mountain or his little hill.*"

And that was all.

"Do you make anything of it?" I inquired at last.

"No," said. Whippet. "No."

I read it through again.

"Who's the 'he'?" I asked.

Whippet blinked at me. "One can't really say, can one? I took it to be the mole. 'His little hill,' you know."

Janet laughed. "I suppose you both know what you're talking about?" she said.

Whippet rose. "I fancy I ought to go, now that I've found Campion and cleared all this up. Thank you for allowing me to inflict myself upon you, Miss Pursuivant. You've been most kind."

I let him say good-bye, and then insisted on escorting him to the gates myself.

"Look here, Whippet," I said, as soon as we were out of earshot, "you'll have to explain. What are you doing in this business at all? Why are you here?"

He looked profoundly uncomfortable. "It's that girl, Effie, Campion," he said. "She's got a strong personality, you know. I met her at Pig's funeral, and she sort of collected me. When she wanted me to drive her down here yesterday I came."

It was an unlikely story from anybody but Whippet, but in his case I was rather inclined to accept it.

"Well, what about the letters?" I persisted.

He shrugged his shoulders. "One's supposed to tear up anonymous letters, isn't one?" he said. "Tear 'em up or keep 'em as mementoes, or frame 'em. Anything but take them seriously. And yet, you know, when they go on and on one seems to come to a point when one says to oneself, 'Who the hell is writing these things?' It's very disturbing, but I like the mole. I shall be at 'The Feathers,' Campion. I give you my word I shall remain there. Look me up when you can spare the time, and we'll go into it. Good-bye."

I let him go. Talking to him, it seemed impossible that he should have the energy to involve himself very deeply in anything so disturbing as our case.

Walking back to the rose garden, I thought about the mole seriously for the first time. A great deal of what Whippet had said about anonymous letters was true. Hayhoe was an educated man, and so was Bathwick, but, even so, why should either of them send both to me and Whippet? It seemed inexplicable.

Janet came to meet me. She was not pleased.

"I don't want to interfere," she said, using the tone and the phrase to mean its exact opposite, "but I don't think you ought to allow her to annoy poor Bathwick."

"Who?" I said, momentarily off my guard.

Janet flared. "Oh, how you irritate me," she said. "You know perfectly well who I mean...that wretched, stupid little girl, Effie Rowlandson. It's bad enough to bring her down here to our village, without letting her get her claws into people who couldn't possibly look after themselves. I hate to have to talk to you like this, Albert, but really you know it is rather disgusting of you."

I was not going to be dragged into a defence of Effie Rowlandson, but I was tired and I resented Bathwick being held up to me as an example of the innocent lamb.

"My dear girl," I said, "you heard about Bathwick getting wet last night. He told Leo an absurd story about falling into a dyke on his way home. However, it took him nearly two hours to get out and on to the main road again, and I'm afraid he'll have to explain himself now that Harris's body has turned up—er—where it has."

I was not looking at her as I spoke, and her little cry brought me round to face her. Her cheeks were crimson and her eyes wide and alarmed.

"Oh!" she said. "Oh! Oh! How terrible!"

And then before I could stop her she had taken to her heels and fled back to the house. I followed her, of course, but she had shut herself in her bedroom, and once more I was given furiously to think.

I went into the library, which is a large, old-fashioned room hardly ever used by the Pursuivants. It was cool and the air was aromatic with the smell of paper. I sat down in a big leather armchair to think things out, and I am afraid that my lack of sleep the night before was too much for me. I woke up to find Janet standing before me. She was pale but determined.

"I thought you'd gone out," she said breathlessly. "It's late, you know. Look here, Albert, I've got to tell you something. I can't let Bathwick get into trouble for something he didn't do, and I know he'd rather die than tell you himself. If you laugh, I'll never speak to you again."

I got up and shook off the remnants of sleep. She looked very charming in her white dress, her eyes defiant.

"I've never felt less like laughing in my life," I said truthfully. "What's all this about Bathwick?"

She took a deep breath. "Mr. Bathwick didn't fall in a dyke," she said. "He fell in our lily-pool."

"Really? How do you know?"

"I pushed him," said Janet in a small voice.

Pressed to continue, she explained:

"Last night, after you took Miss Rowlandson home, I didn't go to bed immediately. I went out on the balcony leading from my room. It was a very bright night, as you know, and I saw someone wandering about in the rose garden. I thought it was Daddy mooching about, worrying over the case, and I went out to talk to him. When I got there it was Bathwick. We walked round the garden together, and when we were quite near the lily-pool he—er—"

She paused.

"Offered you his hand and heart in a slightly too forthright manner?" I suggested.

She nodded gratefully. "I pushed him away, and unfortunately he overbalanced and fell in the pool. As soon as I saw he was safe on land again I went back to the house. It seemed the nicest thing to do. I don't have to tell anybody else, do I?"

"No," I murmured. "No, I don't think so."

She smiled at me. "You're all right really, Albert," she said.

And then, of course, I was called to the telephone. It was Poppy on the end of the wire. She has never grown quite used to the instrument, and I had to hold the receiver some inches away from my ear before I could get her message.

"I've made those inquiries," she boomed. "I don't think the V. came back; anyway, no one saw him. But who do you think was seen roaming about the top storey yesterday morning? My dear, I wouldn't have thought it of him. He seemed so *genuine*. Who? Oh, didn't I tell you? Why, the uncle, *Hayhoe*, of course. Trotting round as though the place belonged to him. The girl who saw him naturally thought I'd given him permission. You never can tell with people, can you?"

CHAPTER 13

Scarecrow in June

JANET WAS AT MY side when I hung up the receiver. "What is it?" she said anxiously. "That was Poppy's voice, wasn't it? Oh, Albert, I'm afraid! Something else terrible has happened."

"Good lord, no!" I said, with an assurance I did not feel. "There's nothing to be frightened of. At least, I don't think so."

She stood looking up at me.

"You know it's all right about Bathwick now, don't you?"

"Of course," I assured her cheerfully. "I'd better go, though. There's something rather important to be fixed, something that's got to be done pretty quickly."

Lugg brought round the car and we went down to the Police Station together. Leo was still there in consultation with Pussey and I was sorry to see him so drawn and haggard. The affair was getting him down. There were deep lines in his face, and his bright eyes were darker than usual in their anxiety. I stated my case.

"Arrest Heigh-ho?" he said. "Really? I don't think we can arrest him, don't you know. We can bring him in and question him—wanted to in the beginnin'—but we can't hold him. There's not a tittle of solid evidence against the feller."

I didn't like to annoy him but I was desperately anxious.

"You must hold him, sir," I said. "That's the whole point. Pull him in for something else."

Leo looked aghast. "Trump up a charge?" he said. "Monstrous!"

There was not time to explain, and I had no proof anyway.

"At least keep him here for twenty-four hours," I pleaded.

Leo frowned at me. "What's got on your mind, my boy?" he enquired. "Sound apprehensive. Anythin' in the wind?"

"I don't know," I said, trying not to appear as rattled as I felt. "Let's go and get him anyway."

Leaving Leo to ponder over the question of arrest, Pussey and I went down in the Lagonda to Mrs. Thatcher's cottage. We picked up young Birkin leaning against a fence on the opposite side of the road. He was a pleasant, shy youth in dilapidated khaki and he made his report in a stage whisper.

"He's been in all the day," he said. "That's 'is room where the light is. You can see 'im if you look."

He pointed to a blurred shadow on the faded chintz curtains and my heart sank. Birkin, I saw, was destined to confine his attentions to dog licences for some time to come. It was a coat and a bolster over the back of a chair, of course.

Pussey stood looking at it when we got into the stuffy little attic bedroom and his language was restrained and almost dignified.

The unfortunate Birkin rather enjoyed it, I fancy. In his private opinion it was a wonderful clever trick and something to tell the lads of the village.

Mrs. Thatcher, a poor old woman who had been too busy all her life to have had time to develop an intelligence, was obstinately mystified. She had told Johnny Birkin that her lodger was in his room, and she honestly thought he was. He must have come downstairs in his stockinged feet, she reckoned. That was all we had to help us.

My scalp was rising. "We've got to find him," I said. "Don't you see it's desperately important?"

Pussey came out of his trance with alacrity.

"Well, he can't have gone far," he said. "This ain't a busy place. Someone will have seen him, bound to."

From Birkin's evidence the curtains had been drawn just after dusk and he had sat there peacefully watching the light ever since. It gave Hayhoe about an hour, and my spirits rose a little.

To do Pussey justice, he mobilized his small force with speed and efficiency. Leo and I had a meal at "The Swan" while they got busy. There were not many methods of exit from Kepesake and, since Mr. Hayhoe did not possess a car, it seemed certain that we should get news of him within an hour or two.

I confess I was jumpy. I felt helpless. My own use in the search was practically nil. I was a comparative stranger, and as such did not inspire the confidence of the suspicious East-Anglian.

We went down to "The Feathers" to interview Whippet and found him dining in the company of Effie Rowlandson and Bathwick. Leo was flabbergasted, and I was surprised myself—they were an odd trio.

When judiciously questioned, it became evident that they knew nothing about Hayhoe, but they looked so much like conspirators that I could have borne to stay and chat with them, had I not been so beset by the fear in my mind.

Round about eleven, Leo, Pussey, and I had a conference. We sat round the stuffy little chargeroom at the Station and Pussey put the case before us.

"He didn't leave by a bus and he didn't hire a car, and if he went on foot by any of the main roads he moves a deal faster than any ordinary animal." He paused and eyed us.

"Seems like that's unnatural he ain't been seen at all," he said. "It isn't as though any strange car 'as been seen goin' through the village. We ain't on the road to anywhere here. It's been a quiet evening, everyone sittin' out on their doorsteps. Can't understand it, unless 'e's took to the fields."

I thought of the warm leafy darkness which surrounded us, of the deep meadows and grass-grown ditches, and I was afraid.

Leo was inclined to be relieved. "Seems to pin it on to him, this boltin'," he said. "Extraordinary thing! Took a dislike to the feller the moment I set eyes on him. Must have been skulkin' in the house all yesterday mornin'. Amazin'."

I didn't know whether to relieve his mind or enhance his fears and I kept silent. Pussey seemed to catch his superior officer's mood.

"Ah well, we'll get him sure enough," he said. "Now we know as who we're lookin' for we won't let 'im go. The whole village is on the look-out for 'im and none of us 'ere won't rest tonight. You go back to your bed, sir. You can leave 'im to us."

It seemed the only thing to do, but I was loth to go.

"You've searched that hill-top?" I said.

"Every inch of it, sir. There's 'is telescope up there but nothin' else. Besides, 'e couldn't get there without bein' seen. 'E's got to come right through the village street with every man on the look-out for 'im. No no, you won't find 'im on that hill-top—'lest 'e's a mowle."

I started, and I suppose my face betrayed me, for he explained in deference to my city training.

"They mowles, they travel underground," he said, and I felt suddenly sick.

Before we left he brought up a matter which had gone clean out of my mind.

"That young lady," he began, "if she could identify...?"

"In the morning," I said hastily. "There'll be a lot to do in the morning."

"Ah ha, you're right, sir," he agreed. "There'll be plenty if we catch un."

"There'll be more if you don't," I said and I went home with Leo.

I was climbing into bed for the first time for forty-eight hours when Pepper appeared with a telephone, which he plugged in by my bed.

"Doctor Kingston," he said, and added, half in commiseration, half in reproach, "at *this* hour, sir..."

Kingston was not only awake but aggressively bright and eager.

"Hope I didn't disturb you," he said. "I've been ringing up all the evening. I was down in the village on a case just after dinner and found the whole place seething. I hear you've got your man on the run. There's nothing I can do, I suppose?"

"I'm afraid not," I said, trying to keep polite.

"Oh, I see." He seemed genuinely disappointed. "I must apologize for being so inquisitive, but you know how it is. I feel I've got a sort of natural interest. You will let me know if anything happens or if I can possibly be of any use, won't you?"

"I will," I said, but he did not ring off.

"You sound tired. Don't overdo it. Oh I say, there's some funny people staying at 'The Feathers.' Strangers. The village doesn't know if it's just a case of ordinary immorality or if there's more to it. The fellow's name is Greyhound, or something. Like 'em looked into?"

I cursed him for his dull life.

"They're spies of mine," I said.

"What? I didn't quite catch you..."

"Spies," I said. "Mine. I've got 'em everywhere. Good night."

I was awake at six. Lugg called me, protestingly.

"Conscientious, aren't you?" he said derisively. "Ayhoe's running away from a pack of narks who want to jug 'im for murder, but he's not going to pass up the little appointment 'e's made with you—Oh dear me no! I don't think."

"All the same I think I'll go," I said. "You never know."

He stood before me, disconsolate, in an outrageous dressing-gown.

"I'll come with you if you like," he offered magnanimously. "There's nothing I like better than a long country walk before the dew's off the grass—cools me feet."

I sent him back to bed, dressed, and went out. It was one of those fine, clear mornings which promise great heat in the day to come. The sky was opal and the grass was soft and springy underfoot.

I went round by the field path and passed down the village street where I caught a glimpse of the ingenuous Birkin. He gave me the news, or rather, the smiling information that there was none.

"We'll be able to get 'im sure enough now the sun's up," he said. "We'll bring 'im back kicking."

I shivered although the morning was warm.

"I hope so," I said and went on.

The little sunken lane was deserted and it was a pleasant morning for walking, but I found my feet lagging and I entered the hill meadow with the deepest foreboding.

It was a longer climb to the top than I had thought and when I reached the summit I was momentarily relieved. It was clear and bare and I disturbed nothing but a brace of larks resting in the short grass. The old brass telescope was still mounted on its tripod. There was dew on the lenses and I wiped them with my handkerchief.

From where I stood I had a stupendous view of the surrounding country. I could see Halt Knights lying rose-red and gracious on the grey saltings, the river mouth, dazzling in the morning sun, and around it, the little pocket hand-kerchief fields and meadows, the corn high and green, the pasture browned a little by the hot weather. It was a lovely county.

Here and there little farms were dotted and among them the white ribbons of the roads twirled and turned.

I stood there for a long time looking at the scene. It was so peaceful, so quiet, and so charming. There was nothing out of place, nothing frightening or remarkable.

And then I saw it. About half a mile away, in the midst of a field waist high in green corn, there was a dilapidated scarecrow, a grotesque, unnatural creature set up to terrify the not-quite-so-clever rooks.

But about this particular effigy there was a difference. Far from being frightened, the rooks were swarming upon it.

I looked through the telescope and straightened myself a moment or so later, sick and giddy, my worst fears realized. Mr. Hayhoe had been found.

CHAPTER 14

The Man They Knew

HE HAD A WOUND in his neck, a strong deep thrust over the collar-bone which had severed the jugular, and when we found him he was not pretty to look at.

Pussey and Leo and I stood round the terrible thing hoisted on a piece of broken paling, and the green corn whispered around us.

After the usual preliminaries, the police brought Hayhoe down on a tumbril to the little mortuary behind the Station, and yet another trestle table was prepared there to receive him.

Leo looked pale and shaken, and Pussey, who had been turned up physically by the first sight of my discovery, presented a mottled ghost of his former cherubic self.

When we were alone together in the mortuary shed, standing between the two white-covered things which had come to upset so violently the time-honoured peace of Kepesake, Leo turned to me.

"This is what you were afraid of?" he said, accusingly.

I looked at him helplessly. "It did go through my mind that something like this might happen. He conveyed that he had definite information, you see."

He passed his hand over his sparse grey hair.

"But who? Who's done it, Campion?" he exploded. "Don't you see, my boy, a terrible thing is happening. It's the *strangers* who are getting killed off. The field's narrowing down to our own people. Good God! What's to be done now?"

"There's not much to go on," I pointed out. "The cornfield was bordered by the road, so the murderer would not have far to carry him even if he had to, although of course there's a chance he was killed on the spot. There was a great deal of blood about."

Leo avoided my eyes. "I know," he murmured. "I know. But what was the feller doing out in the middle of a cornfield with a murderer?"

"Having a very quiet private interview," I said. "I should like an opinion on this wound."

"You shall have it, my boy, you shall have it. The best in the world. Professor Farringdon will be along this morning to see the—ah—other body. This is frightful, Campion—I'm sorry I couldn't get someone at work on him yesterday, but Farringdon was unobtainable, and I didn't want to drag the Home Office into it if I could help it. This makes all the difference, though. 'Pon my soul, I don't know what I ought to do."

Any helpful suggestion I might have made was cut short by the return of Pussey, who had Kingston in tow. The doctor was excited and ashamed of himself for showing it. My opinion of him as a medical man went down a little as he made a cursory examination of Hayhoe. He was anxious to help and yet loth to commit himself by giving a definite opinion.

"I don't know what it was done with," he said at last. "Something narrow and sharp. A dagger, perhaps. One of those old-fashioned things—a trophy."

I glanced at Leo, and from the expression on his face I knew he was thinking of the fearsome array of native weapons on the walls of the billiard-room at Halt Knights. All the same, I didn't see Poppy in the middle of the night in a cornfield with a dagger; that idea seemed to me farfetched and absurd.

Pussey seemed to find Kingston's guesses unsatisfactory, and he got rid of him in the end, but with considerable tact.

"It seems like we'd better leave that to the Professor," he murmured to me. "Wonderful clever old man, the Professor. I reckon he'll be over in half an hour or so. I don't know what he'll think on us—two on 'em instead of one," he added naïvely.

Leo turned away, his hands thrust deep into his pockets and his chin on his breast. We followed him into the station and Pussey made all the necessary arrangements for taking statements, making a search of the place where the body was found, and the important inquiries into Mr. Hayhoe's past history.

The routine work seemed to soothe Leo.

"I suppose we ought not to have moved him from the spot," he said, "until Farringdon arrived. But there seemed no point in leavin' the feller out in the sun hitched up on a spike like that. It was indecent. There's a brutal obviousness about these crimes, Campion. 'Pon my soul, I can't conceive the mind that arranged 'em—anyway, not among my own friends."

"Ah-h, there's still strangers about," said Pussey, with the intention of comforting him. "Likely there'll be *someone* who's had blood on's clothes. We'll find un. Don't you worry, sir."

Leo swung away from him and walked over to the window. "Eh!" he said suddenly, "who's this?"

Looking over his shoulder, I saw a sleek chauffeur-driven Daimler pull up outside the cottage gate. A tall thin grey-faced man descended and came hesitantly up to our door. A moment or so later we made the acquaintance of Mr. Robert Wellington Skinn, junior partner of the ancient and respectable firm of solicitors whose name Kingston had given me.

He was a stiff, dignified personage, and he and Leo took to each other immediately, which was fortunate, or the subsequent interview would certainly have taken much longer and been doubly confusing. As it was, Mr. Skinn came to the point in what was for him, I felt sure, record time.

"In view of everything, I thought I'd better come down myself," he murmured. "An affair of this sort in connexion with one of our clients is, I can assure you, most unusual. I received your inquiries yesterday; I read the papers last night; I connected the two names immediately—Peters and Harris. In the circumstances I thought I had better come down myself."

Pussey and I exchanged glances. We were getting somewhere.

"The two men knew each other, then?" I asked.

He looked at me dubiously as though he wondered if I could be trusted.

"They were brothers," he said. "Mr. Harris changed his name for—ah—no doubt very good reasons of his own, and he is comparatively new to our books. Our principal client was his elder brother, Mr. Rowland Isidore Peters, who died in this district last January."

After a certain amount of delay he went with Leo to view the body, and came back a little green. He was also flustered.

"I wouldn't like to commit myself," he murmured. "I saw Mr. Peters once twelve years ago, and I saw Mr. Harris in London this spring. Those were the only two occasions on which I met either. The—ah—dead man I have just seen resembles both. Do you think I could have a glass of water?"

Pussey pressed him to be more exact, and would have taken him back again, but he refused to go.

"Really, I see no point in it," he said. "I think you can take it that, in my opinion, the dead man is Mr. Harris. After all, there's no reason to suppose that it shouldn't be. He called himself Harris down here, did he not?"

We let him cool down, and when he was more at ease I asked him cautiously about the dead man's estate.

"I really couldn't say, without reference to my books," he protested. "I know Mr. Harris received a considerable sum of money under his brother's will. I can let you know the figures tonight. There was personal property, and of course, the insurance, as far as I remember. It all seemed perfectly in order to me at the time."

Pussey was relieved. "Anyway, we've cleared up his identity, that's one thing," he said. "No doubt on it; can get on with the P.M."

Leo and I escorted the solicitor back to his car. The unfortunate man was shaken by his experience, as well he might be, but he was an obliging soul and before he left, he promised to let us know full details of the two estates.

"There's just one thing," I said, as he got into the car. "Who was Mr. Peters insured with? Do you know?"

He shook his head. "I'm afraid I couldn't tell you off-hand. I think it was the Mutual Ordered Life. I'll look it up."

As soon as he had gone I made a suggestion to Leo, and, having got his consent, sent Lugg and a constable down in the car to fetch Miss Effie Rowlandson. They were gone some little time, and when at last they reappeared they brought not only the girl herself but Bathwick also, which was surprising. There was a considerable delay at the gate, and I went out. The vicar had got over his unexpected friendliness towards me of the night before, and I was aware that all his old antagonism had returned.

"I'm only doing what I'm told, sir," I heard the constable protesting as I came up. 'Besides, the young lady suggested it 'erself only the night before last."

Bathwick ignored him and turned to me.

"This is an outrage," he said. "A young girl subjected to a disgusting sight just to satisfy a few inefficient policemen...I must protest against it; I really must!"

Effie smiled at him wanly. "It's very nice of you, I'm sure," she said, "but I've made up my mind to it; I have, really. You wait here for me," she added.

However he was not to be soothed. He protested so much and so vigorously that my interest in him revived, and I wondered what conceivable purpose he could have in making such a fuss.

In the end we left him in the car, and I took the girl into the little mortuary once more. I was never exactly attracted by Effie Rowlandson, but on that occasion I admired her pluck. She was not callous, and the shock must have been considerable, but she kept her head and played her part with dignity.

"Yes," she said huskily, as I drew the sheet over the limp

form once more. "Yes, it is Roly. I wasn't in love with him, but I'm sorry he's dead. I—"

Her voice broke, and she began to cry. She controlled herself within a moment or so, however, and when I took her back to the bewildered Pussey she made her statement.

"I met him a little over a year ago," she said. "He had a flat in Knightsbridge, and he used to take me out a lot. We got engaged, or nearly engaged, and then—oh, Mr. Campion, you know the rest. I've told you."

Between us we got the story down on paper, and I took her back to the car. Bathwick had climbed out and was waiting for her at the gate. I suppose he saw that she had identified Harris from our faces, for he did not speak to me but, taking her arm, hurried her down the road towards "The Feathers."

Lugg looked after him. "Funny bloke," he said. "Now, where 'ave you got to?"

"An impasse," I said truthfully, and went back to Pussey.

We worked it out while we waited for Professor Farringdon. Pussey put his deductions in a reasonable if not too tidy nutshell.

"There's impersonation been going on," he said judicially. "Sounds like the old story—the good brother and the bad brother. We'll call 'em Peters and Harris for the sake of simplicity. Peters had the money, and on occasions Harris used to impersonate him; well, that's been done before. Harris carried on with this little bird under the name of Peters so that if she should look him up or make inquiries she'd find out he was a man of substance. As for the solicitor, he was in a proper muddle, poor gentleman. The two brothers doubtless looked powerful alike to begin with, and of course that poor bloke in there doesn't look like anything now. What would you say, sir?"

I hesitated. It is never safe to identify a man after twenty-five years, and Kingston had told me that his patient resembled Harris considerably. On the whole, I was inclined to back the Inspector's theory, with one exception. When he talked of the "good brother" and the "bad brother" as Peters and Harris, I thought he should have reversed the names.

I told him so, and he eyed me. "Very likely," he said, "but that doesn't get us any nearer, does it? Who's done the murders? That's what I'd like to know. "

We stood for a moment in silence looking at one another, and the Professor's arrival took us by surprise. He came bustling in, a vigorous little Scotsman with short tufty grey hair and the shrewdest grey-blue eyes I have ever seen.

"Good morning, Inspector," he said. "You've got a remarkable amount of bodies, I hear."

His cheerfulness was disconcerting, and we escorted him to the shed in the yard in silence. As he pored over the man who had called himself Harris, however, his good humour changed, and he turned to me with a very grave face.

"I heard from Sir Leo what you were suggesting, and I take ma hat off to you," he said. "It's a diabolical thing—a diabolical thing."

"Then you think—?" I began.

He waved me silent.

"I wouldn't dare to give an opeenion without a very careful autopsy," he said, "but I wouldn't be at all surprised if you were right; I wouldn't at all."

I walked over to the other side of the room while he was very busy. At last he straightened his back.

"Have it sent round to me," he said, "and I'll let you know

for certain in a day or two. But I think I dare express an opinion—a very tentative one, you understand—that he met his death some little time before he had yon crack over the head."

I put a question and he nodded to me.

"Oh aye," he said, "it was poison. Chloral hydrate, I wouldn't wonder. That"—he indicated the terrible indentation of the skull—"that was in the nature of a blind. You've got a clever man up against you, Mr. Campion. Now let's have a look at the other puir feller."

CHAPTER 15

Lugg Gives Notice

For TWO DAYS THINGS hung fire; that is to say, for two days we were left in peace—Leo to struggle up from beneath the blow, and Pussey and I to collect what useful scraps of information we could.

The village was bright-eyed and uncommunicative. People went to bed early behind locked doors, and sightseers who came to gape at the corner of the field where the wretched Hayhoe had been found were sent hastily on their way by outraged country folk.

Janet developed a strained expression, Poppy took to her bed, and even Whippet was more solicitous than I had supposed possible. He drifted up to see me at odd hours of the day, and sat looking at me in inquiring silence until I packed him off to talk to Janet, who was kind enough to put up with him.

Kingston, of course, was very much in the foreground, and

I even found him useful. He was an inveterate gossip, and the laws of libel and slander had no terrors for him.

The first piece of concrete information came from Mr. Skinn, the solicitor. The Peters who had died in the Tethering nursing home, it transpired, had not been a poor man, and had also had the perspicacity to insure himself for twenty thousand pounds with the Mutual Ordered Life Endowment. His intention, so Mr. Skinn said, had been to borrow upon this policy in order to further some business scheme which he had on hand. As it happened, it had turned out very well indeed for brother Harris.

Concerning Harris we found out very little. He had rented a flat in Knightsbridge under the name of Peters, but he had never been a wealthy man. Our difficulties were enhanced by the confusion in the actual identities of the two men: which was Harris and which was Peters?

In the end I went to Leo. He was sitting in his gun-room, staring mournfully at his magnificent collection of sporting trophies, a mass of papers lying disregarded on his desk.

"We've got ten days, my dear feller," he said at last. "The two inquests have been adjourned to give us a breathing space, don't y'know, but that means we've got to get results. There's a lot of talk already. I don't mind telling you, my boy, the feeling round about is that I ought to have called in Scotland Yard at the first. It seemed simple at the beginning, but now, 'pon my soul, I don't know where things are leading. Every morning I wake up wondering what the day's going to bring forth. We've got a killer at large in the village. God knows where he's going to strike next."

He paused, and when I did not speak he looked at me sharply.

"I've known you since you were a child," he said, "and I know there's somethin' on your mind. If you know anythin' and you're waitin' for proof, don't hesitate to tell me your suspicions. I think I could bear anythin' rather than this uncertainty. Can you make any sense out of this puzzle?"

After working with Leo I knew that he was the most eminently trustworthy man in the world, but I hesitated to commit myself just then. It was too dangerous.

"Look here, Leo," I said, "I know how the first murder was done, and I think I know who did it, but at this stage proof is absolutely impossible, and without proof we can do nothing. Give me a day or two longer. "

He was inclined to be annoyed at first, and I thought he was going to exercise his authority and force my confidence, but he quietened down at last, and I made my next request.

"Can you get a Home Office order for the exhumation of R. I. Peters, who was buried in the Tethering churchyard last January?"

He looked very grave. "I could try," he said at last. "But, my dear fellow, identification after all this time…" He grimaced and threw out his hands.

"I don't know," I persisted. "There are certain circumstances which make rather a lot of difference in that sort of thing."

He frowned at me. "Antimony in the body?" he suggested.

"Not necessarily," I said. "It's a question of the soil, mostly." In the end I got my own way, and afterwards I went out to find Kingston.

He was at home, I discovered by telephone, and Lugg and I went up. He received us in his uncomfortable consulting-room with frank delight.

"Lord! You must be having an off day if you come up and see me," he said reproachfully. "Can I get you a drink?"

"No," I said. "Not now. This is hardly a social call. I want a bit of help."

His round pink face flushed with pleasure.

"Really?" he said. "That's very flattering. I had rather begun to feel that I was in the way down there, don't you know. As a matter of fact, I've been conducting a little private inquiry on my own. That's a most mysterious fellow staying down at 'The Feathers.' Do you know anything about him?"

"Not much," I said truthfully. "I knew him a long while ago—we were at school together, as a matter of fact but I haven't seen him much since."

"Ah!" He wagged his head mysteriously. "Mrs. Thatcher says he used to come to see Hayhoe in the early part of the week. Did you know that?"

I hadn't, of course, and I thanked him.

"I'll look into it," I said. "Meanwhile, you wouldn't like to take me round your churchyard?"

He was only too anxious, and we left the great barrack of a house, which seemed servantless and neglected. He seemed conscious of its deficiencies, and explained in a shame-faced fashion.

"I manage with a man from the village when I haven't any patients," he said. "He's a good fellow, a sort of general odd job man, the son of the local builder, for whom he works when he's not being sexton or my charwoman. When I do get a patient, of course, I have to import a nurse and housekeeper."

We had wandered on ahead of Lugg, and he turned and grimaced at me.

"It's not much of a practice," he said, "otherwise, I suppose, I shouldn't find time for things to be so terribly dull."

As we passed the Lagonda, which was practically new, he looked at it a little wistfully, and I was sorry for him. There was something half childish in his unspoken envy. He had a genius for wasting time, and we spent some moments looking at it. He admired the engine, the gadgets, and the polish on the body-work, and quite won Lugg's heart.

In fact we all got on very well together, and, being in the mood for a confidant at the time, I took the risk and transferred the honour which I had been reserving for Whippet to himself. We talked about the soil of the churchyard. He was interesting and helpful.

"Yes," he said, "it's dry and it's hard, or there's some sort of preservative in it, I think, because I know old Witton, the grave-digger, dragged me out one morning to see a most extraordinary thing. He had opened a three-year-old grave to put in a relation of the dead woman, and somehow or other the coffin lid had become dislodged, and yet there was the body practically in a perfect state of preservation. How did you guess?"

"It's the cow-parsley," I said. "You often find it growing in soil like that."

We went on talking about the soil for some time, and he suddenly saw the drift of my questioning.

"An exhumation?" he said. "Really? I say! That'll be rather—"

He stopped, suppressing the word "jolly," I felt sure.

"—exciting," he added, after a pause. "I've never been present at an exhumation. Nothing so startling ever happens down here."

"I can't promise," I protested. "Nothing's fixed, and for

heaven's sake shut up about it. The one thing that's really dangerous at this stage is gossip."

"It's a question of identification, I suppose?" he said eagerly. "I, say, Campion, you've got a very good chance. What a miracle he chose this particular place to die in! In ninety-nine cemeteries out of a hundred, you know…"

"Yes, but be quiet," I said. "Don't talk about it, for heaven's sake."

"I won't," he promised. "My dear old man, you can rely on me. Besides, I don't see a soul to talk to."

We got away from him eventually, having discovered what we wanted to know, and he stood watching us until we disappeared down the hill. Lugg sighed.

"Lonely life," he observed. "When you see a bloke like that it makes you feel you'd like to take him on a pub-crawl, don't it?"

"Does it?" I said.

He frowned. "You're getting so lah-di-dah and don't-speak-to-me-I'm-clever, you make me tired," he complained. "If I was in your position I wouldn't waste me time muckin' round with corpses. I'd ask a fellow like that up to Town for a week and show 'im the sights."

"My God," I said, "I believe you would."

He chose to be offended, and we drove home in silence.

The following day, which was the third since Hayhoe had been found, I woke up with a sensation that was half exhilaration and half apprehension. I had a premonition that things were going to move, although had I known in what direction I don't think I should have dared to go on.

It began with Professor Farringdon's report. He came over while I was at the station with Pussey, and made it verbally.

"Aye, it was chloral hydrate," he said, "as I told you. It was verra deeficult to decide just how much the man had taken before his death. So there is no way of knowing, you see, whether when yon stone crashed down on his head he was already dead, or if he was merely under the influence of the drug."

Pussey and I both knew the peculiar properties of chloral hydrate; it is a very favourite dope among con-men, but we let him tell us all over again.

"It'd make him very sleepy, you understand. That's why it's so diabolically useful. If ye came upon a man suffering from a slight attack of this poison, ye'd simply think he was in a deep natural sleep."

Pussey looked at me. "All the time he was sitting in that chair, I reckon he was just waiting for the thing to fall upon him, helpless, unable to move. Ah! that's a terrible thing, Mr. Campion."

The Professor went on to dilate upon the fate of Mr. Hayhoe.

"Yon was an interesting wound," he said. "Remarkably lucky, or delivered by someone who was no fool. It caught him just over the collar-bone, and went straight down into his neck. He must have died at once."

He went on to describe the knife that had been used, and even drew it for us, or at least he drew the blade. Pussey didn't know what to make of it at all, but it fitted in to my theory all right.

I left them together and went on to find Whippet. Neither he nor Effie Rowlandson were at "The Feathers" when I arrived, but presently he came up alone in his little A.C.

"I've been house-hunting," he said. "There's a little villa down the road that interests me. It's empty. I like empty houses. Do you? Whenever I'm in a district I go and look at empty houses."

I let him ramble on for some time, and when I thought he must have tired of the subject I put my question to him suddenly. If I hoped to surprise him I was disappointed.

"Hayhoe?" he said. "Oh yes. Oh yes, Campion, I had several conversations with him. Not a nice fellow; he tried to touch me."

"Very likely," I said. "But what did you talk to him about?"

Whippet raised his head, and I looked into his vague pale blue eyes.

"Natural history I think, mostly," he said. "Flora and fauna, you know."

At that moment another great wedge of the jigsaw slipped into place.

"Some are born blind," I said bitterly. "Some achieve blindness. And some have blindness thrust upon them. Moles come into the first category, don't they?"

He said nothing, but remained quite still, looking out of the window.

I went back to Highwaters, and there the thing I had not foreseen, the thing for which I shall never forgive myself, awaited me.

Lugg had gone.

His suitcase, containing his few travelling things, had vanished, and on my dressing-table, weighted down by an ash-tray, was a crisp new pound note.

CHAPTER 16

The Red Hair

A T FIRST I DID not believe it. It was the one contingency which had never entered my mind, and for a moment I was completely thrown off my balance. I heard myself blethering around like a hysterical woman. Pepper did his best to help me.

"A telephone call came through to you, sir," he said. "I didn't take much notice of it, but I understood it was a London call. Mr. Lugg took it, and some time afterwards he came down the back stairs with a suitcase in his hand. He went down to the village by the field path."

And that was all there was to it. That was all anybody could tell me. The exchange was not helpful. There had been a great many incoming calls. The girl at the Post Office had been run off her feet all day. No, she hadn't listened. Of course not! She never did.

I was beside myself. The question of time was so terribly

important, and every now and again a variation of the ghastly vision which I had seen through the brass telescope rose up before my eyes.

The search began immediately.

Leo was sympathetic, and Janet did her best to be soothing. I had to explain to them all that the pound note meant nothing at all. Doubtless there are menservants who go off at a moment's notice, leaving a week's wages in lieu of warning, but Lugg is not one of them. Besides, he had not been seen in the village, nor at the bus stop. He had disappeared as mysteriously as Hayhoe had done; had wandered off into the fields and had vanished in precisely the same way.

I rang up Kingston. He listened to my excited story with disarming interest.

"I say, Campion!" His voice sounded young over the wire. "I've got an idea. I don't know if you remember it, but I said something to you yesterday. You didn't think much of it at the time—I saw that in your face—but I believe it's going to come in useful now. I'll be over right away."

He was. In less than twenty minutes, he came panting up the drive in second gear, his face pink and his eyes burning with delighted enthusiasm. If it had been anybody but Lugg I could have forgiven him.

We held a consultation on the front lawn.

"It's that chap Whippet," he said. "I've been keeping an eye on him. I know how you feel—old school friends and that sort of thing—but you don't really know him at all, and things have been happening, haven't they? Someone must be behind them."

"Yes, well," I said, impatiently, "go on."

He was a little overwhelmed to find me so receptive, I think, but he hurried on eagerly enough.

"There's a house," he said, "an empty villa which stands all by itself at the end of a partly made-up road. It was the beginning of a building scheme which got stopped when the parish council found out what was happening. Whippet's been down there once or twice. I don't say anything definite, but didn't it occur to you that that fellow Hayhoe must have been killed somewhere other than out in the open field? It's a lonely little place. Just the place for a spot of bother. Let's go down."

There was a great deal in what he said, and I did not want to waste time arguing. I moved over towards his car. He looked a little shamefaced.

"I'm afraid we'd better take yours," he said. "Mine's not very young, you know, and she developed a spot of her usual trouble coming along just now. The oil gets in somewhere and rots up the ignition. That is, unless you can wait while I clean a plug or two?"

I was not in the mood to wait, and I got out the Lagonda. He settled beside me with a little sigh of sheer pleasure at its comfort.

"Straight down the hill," he said, "and first on the left."

We turned out of the village and took the long lonely road which winds up through Tethering and on to Rushberry. Presently we turned again. There was a little beer-house, "The Dog and Fowl," sitting coyly under a bank of elms about half a mile farther on, and as we neared it he touched my arm.

"You're rotting yourself up," he said. "You haven't been sleeping, and now this shock on top of it is getting you down. You'd better stop and have one."

I cursed at the delay, but he insisted and we went in.

It was an unattractive little place, old and incredibly dirty. The bar was a mass of cheap advertising trophies, and the only other customer at the time we entered was a toothless old person with a Newgate fringe.

Kingston insisted on beer. There was nothing like old beer for steadying one, he said, and while the half-wit landlady hambled off to fill our tankards, Kingston interrogated the old man concerning Lugg. He did it very well, all things considered, using the idiom of the county.

The old gentleman could not help us, however. He was short of sight and hard of hearing, so he said, and never took much count of strangers, anyway.

It was after the two greasy tankards had been pushed towards us that Kingston showed me the cottage we were going to investigate. It was just visible from the tiny window of the bar. I could see its hideously new red roof peering out amid a mass of foliage about half a mile away.

"Yes, well, let's get on," I said, for I had no great hopes of finding my unfortunate old friend there and time was getting short.

Kingston rose to the occasion.

"All right," he said. "We won't wait for another."

He drained his tankard and so did I. As I turned away from the bar I stumbled and inadvertently caught the old man's pewter mug with my elbow. Its contents were splattered all over the floor and there was another few minutes' delay while we apologized and bought him another drink.

When I got out to the car I stood for a moment looking down at the steering wheel.

"Look here, Kingston," I said, "d'you think it's really necessary to go to this place?"

"I do, old boy, I do." He was insistent. "It's odd, you know, a stranger hanging about an empty house."

I got in and began to drive. A quarter of a mile up the road the car swerved violently and I pulled up.

"I say," I said a little thickly, "would you drive this thing?"

He looked at me and I saw surprised interest on his round, unexpectedly youthful face.

"What's the matter, old man?" he said. "Feeling tired?"

"Yes," I said. "That stuff must have been frightfully strong. Drive on as quick as you can."

He climbed out, and I moved heavily over into the place he had vacated. A minute later we were roaring down the road again. I was slumped forward, my head on my chest, my eyes half closed.

"Can't understand it," I. said, my words blurred. "Got to get ol' Lugg. I'm tired—terribly tired."

I was aware of him pulling up, and through my half-closed eyes I saw a dilapidated little villa, its white stucco streaked with many rains. At the side of the house there was a garage with a badly made little drive of a yard or so leading up to it.

I was aware of Kingston unlocking the doors of this garage and then I was down at the bottom of the car, my eyes closed and my breath coming at long regular intervals.

Kingston stepped behind the steering wheel again and we crawled into the narrow garage. I heard him stop and then I heard him laugh. It was like no sound I had ever heard from him before.

"Well, there you are, my clever Mr. Campion," he said. "Sleep sound."

I think he must have pulled on some gloves, for I was aware of him wiping the steering wheel, and then he dragged me up and pressed my hands upon its smooth surface. He was talking all the time.

"Carbon monoxide is an easy death," he said. "That's why suicides choose it so often. It's so simple, isn't it? I just leave you in the car with the engine running, and close the garage doors as I go out and the neurotic Mr. Campion has done the inexplicable once again. Suicide of distinguished London criminologist."

He was some time completing his arrangements and then, when everything was set, he bent forward.

"I was too clever for you," he said, and there was a rather shocking note in his voice. "Too damned clever."

"By half," I added suddenly and leapt at him.

I hadn't spilt our poor old bearded friend's beer at the "Dog and Fowl" for nothing. Showing a man something interesting out of a window while you put a spot of chloral hydrate in his tankard is poor chaff to catch old birds.

I caught him by the back of the neck and for a moment we grappled. What I hadn't realized, however, was the fellow's strength. Outwardly he appeared a rather flaccid type, but when we came to grips there was muscle there and weight to back it up. Besides, he was demented, he fought like a fiend. I had no longer any doubts about the identity of the hand which had sent that skilful thrust into Hayhoe's neck.

I struggled out of the car, but he was between me and the garage door. I saw his great shoulders hunched against the light. He leapt on me and we fell to the ground. I caught a glimpse of his eyes, and if ever I saw the "blood light" in a man's face it was then. I nearly escaped him once, and had almost reached the doors when something like a vice seized me by the throat. I was lifted bodily and my head crashed down upon the concrete floor.

It was like going down very suddenly in a lift. It went on and on and at the end there was darkness.

I came up again painfully, in little jerks. I was aware that my arms were moving up and down with a slow rhythmic motion I could not control, and then I was gasping, fighting for breath.

"Look out—look out. You're doing nicely. Don't get excited. Steady yourself."

The voice came to me like a dream, and I saw through the fog a ridiculous small boy with ink smeared all over his face looking down at my bed in the sicker. Then the boy disappeared, but I still saw the same face, although the ink had been removed. It was Whippet. He was kneeling behind me giving me artificial respiration.

The whole business came back with a rush.

"Lugg!" I said. "My God, we've got to get Lugg!"

"I know." Whippet's voice sounded almost intelligent. "Fellow's positively dangerous, isn't he? I let Kingston get away before I got you out. I mean, I didn't want to have two of you on my hands."

I sat up. My head was throbbing and there was only one clear thought in my mind.

"Come on," I said. "We've got to get him before it's too late."

He nodded, and I was suddenly grateful for the understanding in his face.

"A fellow came by on a bicycle a moment or so ago," he said. "I put it to him and sent him off down to the village. He's going to send the whole crowd up to the nursing home. I thought that was the best way. I've got my car in the meadow round the back. Let's go to Tethering straight away, shall we?"

I don't remember the journey to Tethering. My head felt as though it was going to burst, my mouth was like an old rat-trap, and I couldn't get rid of a terrible nightmare in which Lugg was hoist on a scarecrow stake which was as high as the Nelson Column.

What I do remember is our arrival. We pulled up outside the front door of Kingston's barrack of a house, and when it wouldn't give we put our shoulders to it. I remember the tremendous sense of elation when it shattered open before our combined strength.

It was a movement on the first floor that sent us racing up the stairs, and, since five doors on the landing were open, we concentrated on the one that was not. It was unlocked, but someone held it on the other side. We could hear him snarling and panting as we fought with it.

And then, quite suddenly, it swung back. I was so beside myself that I should have charged in and taken what was coming to me, but it was Whippet who kept his head. He pulled me back and we waited.

Through the open door I could see a bed, and on it there was a large, familiar form. The face was uncovered, and as far as I could see the colour was natural. But as I stared at it I saw the thing that sent the blood racing into my face and turned my body cold with the realization of the thing I had not dreamed.

The faded grey-black fluff which surrounds Lugg's bald patch was as red as henna would make it. I saw the truth, the body of one fat man is much like the body of another once the features are obliterated, and what time can do can be done by other agencies. Kingston was going to have a body for his "jolly" exhumation after all.

I dropped on my hands and knees. Ducking under the blow he aimed at me from his place of vantage behind the door, I caught him by the ankles. I was on his chest with my hands round his throat when I heard the second car pull up and Leo's voice on the stairs.

CHAPTER 17

Late Final

I T TOOK THREE POLICEMEN to get Kingston into the car, and when he came up before the magistrates there was an unprecedented scene in the court. At the Assizes his counsel pleaded insanity, a defence which failed, and I think justifiably; but that was later.

My own concern at the time was Lugg. Whippet and I worked upon him until Pussey got us a doctor from a neighbouring village, who saved him after an uncomfortably stiff fight. It was chloral hydrate again, of course. Kingston was not mad enough not to know what he was doing. He did not want any wound showing in his exhibition corpse. What his "finishing" process was to be, I can only guess, and I do not like to think of it even now.

Lugg told us his story as soon as we got him round. It was elementary. Kingston had simply phoned up Highwaters, made sure from Pepper that I was down in the village, and had then asked for Lugg. To him he gave a message purporting to come from me. According to this, I had work for him to do in town, but I wanted to see him first up at Tethering church-yard, where, Kingston hinted, I had discovered something. Lugg was to pack his bag and nip down the field path to the road to meet Kingston in the car. The pound note was to be left for Pepper in case I could not return. That was all. Lugg fell for the story, Kingston did meet him, and the reason they had not been seen was that the doctor's car was far too well known for anybody to notice it.

On arrival at Tethering, Lugg was left in the dining-room, where he was given beer and told to wait. He drank the beer and the chloral which was in it and mercifully remembered no more.

Kingston must have got him upstairs alone and have just completed the hairdressing process when I phoned.

It was a pretty little trap, and Lugg's comments on it when he considered it are not reportable.

"You done it," he said reproachfully. "How was I to know you was leadin' the bloke up the garden with your 'come-and-'old-me-'and' every five minutes? You stuffed him full of the exhumation, thinking 'e'd go for you, I suppose? Never thought o' me. Isn't that you all over?"

I apologized. "Let's be thankful you're alive to tell the tale," I ventured.

He scowled at me. "I am. Got to shave me 'ead now. What are my London friends goin' to think about that? 'Oliday in the country—Oh, yes, very likely!"

When we reached this point I thought it best to let him sleep, for there was still much to be done.

During the next twenty-four hours we worked incessantly, and at the end of it the case against Kingston was complete.

It was on the evening of the day on which the exhumation had taken place, that Leo and I went down with Janet to Halt Knights. Leo was still simmering from the effects of that grimly farcical ceremony which had welded the final link in our chain of evidence.

"Bricks!" he said explosively. "Yellow bricks wrapped up in a blanket and nailed down in a coffin...' Pon my soul, Campion, the fellow was an impious blackguard as well as a murderer. Even now, I don't see how he did it alone."

"He wasn't alone," I pointed out mildly. "He had Peters to help him, to say nothing of that fellow who worked for him—the builder's son. In country places the builder is usually the undertaker, too, isn't he?"

"Royle!" Leo was excited. "Young Royle...that explains the key of the mortuary. Was the boy in it, do you think?"

"Hardly," I murmured. "I imagine Kingston simply managed him. He says his master offered to measure up the body while he did a repair job in the house. The nurse must have been an accomplice, of course, but we shall never get her. She and Kingston got the death certificate between them."

"You're terribly confusing," Janet cut in from the back of the car. "How many brothers were there?"

"None," I said, "as the clever young man from London suspected after he'd had it thrust well under his nose, poor chap. There was only the one inimitable Pig."

Janet will forgive me, I feel sure, if I say here that she is not a clever girl. On this occasion she was obtuse.

"Why go to all the trouble of pretending he died in January?"

"Because," I said sadly, "of the insurance, my poppet. Twenty thousand pounds... He and Kingston were going to do a deal. Tie up with your medical man and let the Mutual Ordered Life settle your money troubles. Kingston met Pig in town and they hatched the whole swindle up between them. Pig invented a wicked brother and laid the foundations by hoodwinking his own solicitors, who were a stuffy old firm at once reputable enough to impress the insurance company and sufficiently moribund to let Pig get away with his hole-and-corner death."

"Neat," said Janet judicially, and added with that practicalness so essentially feminine, "Why didn't it work?"

"Because of the fundamental dishonesty of the man Pig. He wouldn't pay up. Once he had collected, he knew he had Kingston by the short hairs and, besides, by then the idea of developing this place had bitten him. I fancy he kept his doctor pal on a string, promising him and promising and then laughing at him. What he did not consider was the sort of fellow he had to deal with. Kingston is a conceited chap. He has a sort of blind courage coupled with no sense of proportion. Only a man with that type of mentality could have pulled off his share in the original swindle. The fact that he had been cheated by Pig wounded his pride unbearably, and then, of course, he found the man untrustworthy."

"Untrustworthy?" Leo grunted.

"Well, he began to get drunk, didn't he?" I said. "Think of Kingston's position. He saw himself cheated out of the share of the profits and at the same time at the complete mercy of a man who was in danger of getting too big for his boots, drinking too much, and blowing the gaff. Admittedly, Pig could not give Kingston away without exposing his own guilt, but a man who gets very drunk may be careless. Then there was Hayhoe. The wicked uncle finds the wicked nephew in clover and wishes to browse also. He even instals a telescope on a neighbouring hillside in the hope of keeping an eye on developments at Highwaters. There is another danger for Kingston. I think the whole ingenious business came to him in a flash, and he acted on impulse moved by fury, gingered up by fear."

Leo made an expressive sound. "Terrible feller," he said. "Heigh-ho blackmailed him, I suppose, after guessin' the truth?"

"Uncle Hayhoe was bent on selling his discretion, certainly," I said, "but I don't think even he guessed Kingston had killed Pig. All he knew was that there was something infernally fishy about the first funeral. He made an appointment with Kingston to talk it over and they chose the empty villa to discuss terms. Kingston killed him there and later on carried him to the corn-field where we found him. He left the knife in the wound until he got him *in situ,* as it were; that's how he avoided a great deal of the blood."

Janet shuddered. "He deceived us all very well," she said. "I never dreamed—"

Leo coughed noisily. "Utterly deceived," he echoed. "Seemed a decent enough feller."

"He was amazing," I agreed. "My arrival at dinner that evening must have shaken him up a bit in all conscience, since he'd seen me at the funeral, but he came out with the brother story immediately, and made it sound convincing. The only mistake he made was in moving the body to the river when I said I was going to examine it. He acted on impulse there, you see; he saw his way and went straight for it every time."

Janet drew back. "You ought not to have walked into that last trap he set for you," she said.

"My dear girl," I said, anxious to defend myself, "we had to have proof of murder or attempted murder, for as far as proof was concerned he'd got clean away with his first two efforts. All the same, I don't think I'd have been so foolhardy if it hadn't been for Lugg."

"You'd have looked pretty green if it hadn't been for Gilbert," she said.

I looked at her sharply, and saw that she was blushing.

"Whippet and I had a word or two on the phone after Kingston had agreed to pick me up at Highwaters," I admitted. "He spotted the empty villa and put me on to it. We guessed if there was to be an attempt on me Kingston would take me there. I shouldn't have been so brave without him. Mastermind is fond of life."

Janet dimpled. She is very pretty when her cheeks go pink.

"Then you know about Gilbert?" she said.

I stared at her. "How much do you know?"

"A little," she murmured.

"My hat!" I said.

Leo was on the point of demanding an explanation when we pulled up at the Knights. We found Poppy, Pussey, and Whippet waiting for us in the lounge, and when we were all sitting round with the ice cubes clinking in our tall glasses, Poppy suddenly turned on me.

"I'm sure you've made a mistake, Albert," she said. "I don't want to be unkind, dear, and I do think you're very clever. But how could Doctor Kingston have killed Harris, or Peters as you call him, when he was in this room playing poker with Leo when the vase fell upon him? You said yourself it couldn't have slipped off by accident."

The time had come for me to do my parlour trick, and I did my best to perform it in the ancient tradition.

"Poppy," I said, "do you remember Kingston coming to see your little maid on the morning of the murder? You took him up yourself, I suppose, and you both had a look at the kid? There was some ice in the water jug by her bed, wasn't there?"

She considered. "No," she said. "He came down, and I gave him a drink with ice in it. That was after I'd turned him into the bathroom to wash his hands. I came down here, and he followed me, and after he'd had his drink he took some tablets up to Flossie that he'd forgotten."

"Ah!" I said impressively. "Was he long following you down?"

She looked up with interest. "Why, yes, he was," she said. "Quite a while, now I think of it."

Having located my rabbit, as it were, I proceeded to produce it with a flourish.

"Kingston told us he met Harris, alias Pig, on the stairs, and that Pig had a hangover," I began. "The first wasn't true, the second was. Pig was in his bedroom when Kingston slipped in to see him, having first got rid of you. Pig was dressed, but he wanted a corpse-reviver and he trusted Kingston, never dreaming that he'd goaded the man too far. After all, people don't go about expecting to be murdered. In his doctor's bag Kingston had some chloral, which is a reputable narcotic when used in moderation. He saw his opportunity. He administered a tidy dose, and sent Pig to sit out on the lawn. He followed him downstairs, and through the lounge windows saw him settle down. I think his original intention was to let him die, and to trust the coroner to suspect a chronic case of dope. But this was risky, and the position of the chair, which was directly beneath the window, put the other idea into his head. If you notice, the windows on each floor in this house are directly above those on the last, and no one who knows the place can have missed the stone urns. They were originally intended to obscure the attic windows from the outside. It was while Kingston was drinking his highball that he had his brainwave. There were two or three solid rectangles of ice in his glass, and he pocketed two of them. Then he told you some story about forgotten tablets and went up to the top floor again, which was deserted at that time of the morning. There he discovered that, as he had suspected, Pig was sitting directly beneath the box-room urn. He knew he was unconscious already, and would remain so. The rest was easy. He took the urn out of its socket and balanced it on its peg half over the ledge. Then he blocked it into position with the two pieces of ice, and went directly downstairs. The ledge is just below the level of the window-sill, so the chance of anyone who passed the box-room door noticing that the urn was an inch or so out of place was remote. All he had to do, then, was to wait."

Poppy sat staring at me, her face pale.

"Until the ice melted and the urn fell?" she said. "How—how ghastly!"

Pussey wagged his head. "Powerful smart," he said. "Powerful smart. If I might ask you, sir, how did you come to think of that?"

"The moss on the ledge was damp when I arrived," I said. "The inference did not dawn on me at first, but when I had a highball here the other day I saw the ice and suddenly realized what it meant."

"Wonderful!" said Whippet, without malice. "I was after the same fellow, of course, but the alibi put me out."

Leo stared at him as if he had only just become aware of his existence.

"Mr.—er—Whippet," he said, "very pleased to have you here, of course, my boy. But where do you fit into this extraordinary story? What are you doin' here?"

There was a pause, and they all looked at me as though I was responsible for him. I looked at Whippet.

"His little hands are sore and his snout bleedeth," I said. "This is Gilbert Whippet, Junior, son of Q. Gilbert Whippet, of the Mutual Ordered Life Endowment Company, sometimes called the M.O.L.E. It didn't occur to me until that day at 'The Feathers,' and then I could have kicked myself for missing it. You always were a lazy beast, Whippet."

He smiled faintly. "I—er—prefer writing to action, you know," he said, hesitantly. "I am sorry, Campion, to have dragged you into this, but at the beginning we had nothing to go on at all except a sort of uneasy suspicion. I couldn't very well approach you direct because—well—er—there was nothing direct about it, so I—er—wrote."

His voice trailed away.

"Both Lugg and I appreciated your style," I said.

He nodded gravely. "It seemed the best way to ensure your interest," he said calmly. "Whenever I thought you might be flagging, I wrote again."

"Your people got hold of Effie, and you set her on to me, I suppose?" I said coldly.

"Er—yes," agreed Whippet, without shame.

Poppy glanced round the room. "Where is she now?" she demanded.

Whippet beamed. It was the broadest smile I ever saw on his face.

"With—er—Bathwick," he murmured. "They've gone into the town, to the pictures. Very suitable, I thought. Happy endings and—er—all that."

I gaped at him. He had my respect.

When Lugg and I went back to London the next day, Poppy, who had gone to Highwaters for lunch, stood with Leo and waved good-bye to us from the lawn. The sky was dappled blue and white, the birds sang, and the air smelt of hay.

Janet, with Whippet in tow, came running up to us just before we started. Her eyes were dancing, and she looked adorable.

"Congratulate us, Albert," she said. "We're engaged. Isn't it wonderful?"

I gave them my blessing with a good grace. Whippet blinked at me.

"I'm indebted to you, Campion," he said.

We drove for some time in silence. I was thoughtful and Lugg, who was as bald as an egg, seemed depressed. As we reached the main road he nudged me.

"What a performance!" he said.

"Whose?" I inquired, not above appreciating a little honour where honour was due.

He leered. "That bloke Whippet. Come down to a place with Miss Effie Rowlandson, and go orf with Miss Janet Pursuivant... That took a bit o' doing."

"Lugg," I said sadly, "would you like to walk home?"

Want more Albert Campion? Read on for the first four chapters of:

THE FASHION IN SHROUDS

Albert Campion #10

Coming from Felony & Mayhem in November 2008

CHAPTER 1

PROBABLY THE MOST exasperating thing about the Fashion is its elusiveness. Even the word has a dozen definitions, and when it is pinned down and qualified, as "the Fashion in woman's dress," it becomes ridiculous and stilted and is gone again.

To catch at its skirts it is safest to say that it is a kind of miracle, a familiar phenomenon. Why it is that a garment which is honestly attractive in, say, 1910 should be honestly ridiculous a few years later and honestly charming again a few years later still is one of those things which are not satisfactorily to be explained and are therefore jolly and exciting and an addition to the perennial interest of life.

When the last Roland Papendeik died, after receiving a knighthood for a royal wedding dress—having thus scaled the heights of his ambition as a great couturier—the ancient firm declined and might well have faded into one of the amusing legends Fashion leaves behind her had it not been for a certain phoenix quality possessed by Lady Papendeik.

At the moment when descent became apparent and dissolution likely Lady Papendeik discovered Val, and from the day that the Valentine cape in Lincoln-green facecloth flickered across the salon and won the hearts of twenty-five professional buyers and subsequently five hundred private purchasers Val climbed steadily, and behind her rose up the firm of Papendeik again like a great silk tent.

At the moment she was standing in a fitting room whither she had dragged a visitor who had come on private business of his own and was surveying herself in a wall-wide mirror with earnest criticism.

Like most of those people whose personality has to be consciously expressed in the things they create, she was a little more of a person, a little more clear in outline than is usual. She had no suggestion of overemphasis, but she was a sharp, vivid entity, and when one first saw her the immediate thing one realised was that it had not happened before.

As she stood before the mirror considering her burgundy-red suit from every angle she looked about twenty-three, which was not the fact: Her slenderness was slenderness personified and her yellow hair, folding softly into the nape of her neck at the back and combed into a ridiculous roll in front, could have belonged to no one else and would have suited no other face.

It occurred to her visitor, who was regarding her with the detached affection of a relation, that she was dressed up to look like a female, and he said so affably.

She turned and grinned at him, her unexpectedly warm

grey eyes, which saved her whole appearance from affectation, dancing at him happily.

"I am," she said. "I am, my darling. I'm female as a cart-load of monkeys."

"Or a kettle of fish, of course," observed Mr. Albert Campion, unfolding his long thin legs and rising from an inadequate gilt chair to look in the mirror also. "Do you like my new suit?"

"Very good indeed." Her approval was professional. "Jamieson and Fellowes? I thought so. They're so mercifully uninspired. Inspiration in men's clothes is stomach-turning. People ought to be shot for it."

Campion raised his eyebrows at her. She had a charming voice which was high and clear and so unlike his own in tone and colour, that it gave him a sense of acquisition whenever he heard it.

"Too extreme," he said. "I like your garment, but let's forget it now."

"Do you? I was wondering if it wasn't a bit 'intelligent.'"

He looked interested.

"I wanted to talk to you before these people come. Aren't we lunching alone?"

Val swung slowly round in only partially amused surprise. For a moment she looked her full age, which was thirty, and there was character and intelligence in her face.

"You're too clever altogether, aren't you?" she said. "Go away. You take me out of my stride."

"Who is he? It's not to be a lovely surprise, I trust?" Campion put an arm round her shoulders and they stood for a moment admiring themselves with the bland unselfconsciousness of the nursery. "If I didn't look so half-witted we should be very much alike," he remarked presently. "There's a distinct resemblance. Thank God we took after Mother and not the other side. Red hair would sink either of us, even Father's celebrated variety. Poor old Herbert used to look like nothing on earth."

He paused and considered her dispassionately in the mirror, while it occurred to him suddenly that the relationship between brother and sister was the one association of the sexes that was intrinsically personal.

"If one resents one's sister or even loathes the sight of her," he remarked presently, "it's for familiar faults or virtues which one either has or hasn't got oneself and one likes the little beast for the same rather personal reasons. I think you're better than I am in one or two ways, but I'm always glad to note that you have sufficient feminine weaknesses to make you thoroughly inferior on the whole. This is a serious, valuable thought, by the way. See what I mean?"

"Yes," she said with an irritating lack of appreciation, "but I don't think it's very new. What feminine weaknesses have I got?"

He beamed at her. In spite of her astonishing success she could always be relied upon to make him feel comfortingly superior.

"Who's coming to lunch?"

"Alan Dell—Alandel aeroplanes."

"Really? That's unexpected. I've heard of him, of course, but we've never met. Nice fellow?"

She did not answer immediately and he glanced at her sharply.

"I don't know," she said at last and met his eyes. "I think so, very."

Campion grimaced. "Valentine the valiant."

She was suddenly hurt and colour came into her face.

"No, darling, not necessarily," she objected a little too vehemently. "Only twice shy, you know, only twice, not forever."

There was dignity in the protest. It brought him down to earth and reminded him effectively that she was after all a distinguished and important woman with every right to her own private life. He changed the conversation, feeling, as he sometimes did, that she was older than he was for all her femininity.

"Can I smoke in this clothespress without sacrilege?" he enquired. "I came up here once to a reception when I was very young. The Perownes had it then as their town house. That was in the days before the street went down and a Perowne could live in Park Lane. I don't remember much about it except that there were golden cream horns bursting with fruit all round the cornice. You've transformed the place. Does Tante Marthe like the change of address?"

"Lady Papendeik finds herself enchanted," said Val cheerfully, her mind still on her clothes. "She thinks it a pity trade should have come so near the park but she's consoling herself by concentrating on 'our mission to glorify the Essential Goddess.' This is a temple, my boy, not a shop. When it's not a temple it's that damned draughty hole of Maude Perowne's. But on the whole it's just exactly what she always wanted. It has the grand manner, the authentic Papa Papendeik touch. Did you see her little black pages downstairs?"

"The objects in the turbans? Are they recent?"

"Almost temporary," said Val, turning from the mirror and slipping her arm through his. "Let's go up and wait. We're lunching on the roof."

As he came through the wide doorway from a hushed

and breathless world whose self-conscious good taste was almost over-powering to the upper, or workshop, part of the Papendeik establishment, Mr. Campion felt a gratifying return to reality. A narrow uncarpeted corridor, still bearing traces of the Perowne era in wallpaper and paint, was lit by half-a-dozen open doorways through which came a variety of sounds, from the chiming of cups to the hiss of the pressing iron, while above all there predominated the strident, sibilant chatter of female voices, which is perhaps the most unpleasant noise in the world.

An elderly woman in a shabby navy-blue dress came bustling along towards them, a black pincushion bumping ridiculously on her hipbone as she walked. She did not stop but smiled and passed them, radiating a solid obstinacy as definite as the clatter of her old-lady shoes on the boards. Behind her trotted a man in a costume in which Campion recognised at once Val's conception of the term "inspired." He was breathless and angry and yet managed to look pathetic, with doggy brown eyes and the cares of the world on his compact little shoulders.

"She won't let me have it," he said without preamble. "I hate any sort of unpleasantness, but the two girls are waiting to go down to the house and I distinctly promised that the white model should go with the other. It's the one with the draped corsage."

He sketched a design with his two hands on his own chest with surprising vividness.

"The vendeuse is in tears."

He seemed not far off them himself and Mr. Campion felt sorry for him.

"Coax her," said Val without slackening pace and they

hurried on, leaving him sighing. "Rex," she said as they mounted the narrow uncarpeted staircase amid a labyrinth of corridors. "Tante says he's not quite a lady. It's one of her filthy remarks that gets more true the longer you know him."

Campion made no comment. They were passing through a group of untidy girls who had stepped aside as they appeared.

"Seamstresses," Val explained as they came up on to the landing. "Tante prefers the word to 'workwomen.' This is their room."

She threw open a door which faced them and he looked into a vast attic where solid felt-covered tables made a mighty horseshoe whose well was peopled with dreadful brown headless figures each fretted with pinpricks and labelled with the name of the lady whose secret faults of contour it so uncompromisingly reproduced.

Reflecting that easily the most terrifying thing about women was their practical realism, he withdrew uneasily and followed her up a final staircase to a small roof garden set among the chimney-pots, where a table had been laid beneath a striped awning.

It was early summer and the trees in the park were round and green above the formal flower beds, so that the view, as they looked down upon it, was like a coloured panoramic print of eighteenth-century London, with the houses of the Bayswater Road making a grey cloud on the horizon.

He sat down on a white basketwork settee and blinked at her in the sunlight.

"I want to meet Georgia Wells. You're sure she's coming?"

"My dear, they're all coming." Val spoke soothingly. "Her husband, the leading man, Ferdie Paul himself and heaven knows who else. It's partly mutual publicity and partly a genuine inspection of dresses for *The Lover*, now in rehearsal. You'll see Georgia all right."

"Good," he said and his lean face was unusually thoughtful. "I shall try not to be vulgar or indiscreet, of course, but I must get to know her if I can. Was she actually engaged to Portland-Smith at the time he disappeared, or was it already off by then?"

Val considered and her eyes strayed to the doorway through which they had come.

"It's almost three years ago, isn't it?" she said. "My impression is that it was still on, but I can't swear to it. It was all kept so decently quiet until the family decided that they really had better look for him, and by then she was stalking Ramillies. It's funny you never found that man, Albert. He's your one entire failure, isn't he?"

Apparently Mr. Campion did not care to comment.

"How long has she been Lady Ramillies?"

"Over two years, I think."

"Shall I get a black eye if I lead round to Portland-Smith?"

"No, I don't think so. Georgia's not renowned for good taste. If she stares at you blankly it'll only mean that she's forgotten the poor beast's name."

He laughed. "You don't like the woman?"

Val hesitated. She looked very feminine.

"Georgia's our most important client, 'the best-dressed actress in the world gowned by the most famous couturier.' We're a mutual benefit society."

"What's the matter with her?"

"Nothing." She glanced at the door again and then out over the park. "I admire her. She's witty, beautiful, predatory, intrinsically vulgar and utterly charming."

Mr. Campion became diffident.

"You're not jealous of her?"

"No, no, of course not. I'm as successful as she is—more."

"Frightened of her?"

Val looked at him and he was embarrassed to see in her for an instant the candid-eyed child of his youth.

"Thoroughly."

"Why?"

"She's so charming," she said with uncharacteristic naïveté.

"She's got *my* charm."

"That's unforgivable," he agreed sympathetically. "Which one?"

"The only one there is, my good ape. She makes you think she likes you. Forget her. You'll see her this afternoon. I like her really. She's fundamentally sadistic and not nearly so brilliant as she sounds, but she's all right. I like her. I do like her."

Mr. Campion thought it wisest not to press the subject and would doubtless have started some other topic had he not discovered that Val was no longer listening to him. The door to the staircase had opened and her second guest had arrived.

As he rose to greet the newcomer Campion was aware of a fleeting sense of disappointment.

In common with many other people he cherished the secret conviction that a celebrity should look peculiar, at the very least, and had hitherto been happy to note that a great number did.

Dell was an exception. He was a bony thirty-five-year-old with greying hair and the recently scoured appearance of one intimately associated with machinery. It was only when he spoke, revealing a cultured mobile voice of unexpected authority, that his personality became apparent. He came forward shyly and it occurred to Campion that he was a little put out to find that he was not the only guest.

"Your brother?" he said. "I had no idea Albert Campion was your brother."

"Oh, we're a distinguished family," murmured Val brightly, but an underlying note of uncertainty in her voice made Campion glance at her shrewdly. He was a little startled by the change in her. She looked younger and less elegant, more charming and far more vulnerable. He looked at the man and was relieved to see that he was very much aware of her.

"You've kept each other very dark," said Dell. "Why is that?"

Val was preoccupied at the moment with two waiters who had arrived with the luncheon from the giant hotel next door, but she spoke over her shoulder.

"We haven't. Our professions haven't clashed yet, that's all. We nod to each other in the street and send birthday cards. We're the half of the family that is on speaking terms, as a matter of fact."

"We're the bones under the ancestral staircase."

Campion embarked upon the explanation solely because it was expected of him. It was a reason he would never have considered sufficient in the ordinary way, but there was something about Alan Dell, with his unusually bright blue eyes and sudden smile, which seemed to demand that extra consideration which is given automatically to important children, as if he were somehow special and it was to everyone's interest that he should be accurately informed.

"I was asked to leave first—in a nice way, of course. We all have charming manners. Val followed a few years later, and now, whenever our names crop up at home, someone steps into the library and dashes off another note to the family solicitor disinheriting us. Considering their passion for self-expression, they always seem to me a little unreasonable about ours."

"That's not quite true about me." Val leant across the, table and spoke with determined frankness. "I left home to marry a man whom no one liked, and after I married I didn't like him either. Lady Papendeik, who used to make my mother's clothes, saw some of my designs and gave me a job—"

"Since when you've revolutionised the business," put in Campion hastily with some vague idea of saving the situation. He was shocked. Since Sidney Ferris had died the death he deserved in a burnt-out motorcar with which, in a fit of alcoholic exuberance, he had attempted to fell a tree, he had never heard his widow mention his name.

Val seemed quite unconscious of anything unusual in her behavior. She was looking across at Dell with anxious eyes.

"Yes," he said, "I've been hearing about you. I didn't realise how long Papendeik's had been going. You've performed an extraordinary feat in putting them back on the map. I thought change was the essence of fashion."

Val flushed.

"It would have been easier to start afresh," she admitted. "There was a lot of prejudice at first. But as the new designs were attractive they sold, and the solidarity of the name was a great help on the business side."

"It would be, of course." He regarded her with interest.

"That's true. If the things one makes are better than the other man's, one does get the contracts. That's the most comforting discovery I've ever made."

They laughed at each other, mutually admiring and entirely comprehending, and Campion, who had work of his own to do, felt oddly out of it.

"When do you expect Georgia Wells?" he ventured. "About three?"

He felt the remark was hardly tactful as soon as he had made it, and Val's careless nod strengthened the impression. Dell was interested, however.

"Georgia Wells?" he said quickly. "Did you design her clothes for *The Little Sacrifice?*"

"Did you see them?" Val was openly pleased. Her sophistication seemed to have deserted her entirely. "She looked magnificent, didn't she?"

"Amazing." He glanced at the green treetops across the road. "I rarely go to the theatre," he went on after a pause, "and I was practically forced into that visit, but once I'd seen her I went again alone."

He made the statement with a complete unselfconsciousness which was almost embarrassing and sat regarding them seriously.

"Amazing," he repeated. "I never heard such depth of feeling in my life. I'd like to meet that woman. She had some sort of tragedy in her life, I think? The same sort of thing as in the play."

Mr. Campion blinked. Unexpected naïveté in a delightful stranger whose ordinary intelligence is obviously equal to or beyond one's own always comes as something of a shock. He glanced at Val apprehensively. She was sitting up, her mouth smiling.

"She divorced her husband, the actor, some years ago, and there was a barrister fiancé who disappeared mysteriously a few months before she married Ramillies," she said. "I don't know which incident reminded you of the play."

Alan Dell stared at her with such transparent disappointment and surprise that she blushed, and Campion began to understand the attraction he had for her.

"I mean," she said helplessly, "*The Little Sacrifice* was about a woman relinquishing the only man she ever loved to marry the father of her eighteen-year-old daughter. Wasn't that it?"

"It was about a woman losing the man she loved in an attempt to do something rather fine," said Dell and looked unhappy, as if he felt he had been forced into an admission.

"Georgia was brilliant. She always is. There's no one like her." Val was protesting too much and realising it too late, in Campion's opinion, and he was sorry for her.

"I saw the show," he put in. "It was a very impressive performance, I thought."

"It was, wasn't it?" The other man turned to him gratefully. "It got one. She was so utterly comprehendable. I don't like emotional stuff as a rule. If it's good I feel I'm butting in on strangers, and if it's bad it's unbearably embarrassing. But she was so—so confiding, if you see what I mean. There *was* some tragedy, wasn't there, before she married Ramillies? Who was this barrister fiancé?"

"A man called Portland-Smith," said Campion slowly.

"He disappeared?"

"He vanished," said Val. "Georgia may have been terribly upset; I think she probably was. I was only being smart and silly about it."

Dell smiled at her. He had a sort of chuckleheaded and shy affection towards her that was very disarming.

"That sort of shock can go very deep, you know," he said

awkwardly. "It's the element of shame in it—the man clearing off suddenly and publicly like that."

"Oh, but you're wrong. It wasn't that kind of disappearance at all." Val was struggling between the very feminine desire to remove any misapprehension under which he might be suffering and the instinctive conviction that it would be wiser to leave the subject altogether. "He simply vanished into the air. He left his practice, his money in the bank and his clothes on the peg. It couldn't have been anything to do with Georgia. He'd been to a party at which I don't think she was even present, and he left early because he'd got to get back and read a brief before the morning. He left the hotel about ten o'clock and didn't get to his chambers. Somewhere between the two he disappeared. That's the story, isn't it, Albert?"

The thin young man in the horn-rimmed spectacles did not speak at once, and Dell glanced at him enquiringly.

"You took it up professionally?"

"Yes, about two years later." Mr. Campion appeared to be anxious to excuse his failure. "Portland-Smith's career was heading towards a recordership," he explained, "and at the time he seemed pretty well certain to become a county court judge eventually, so his relatives were naturally wary of any publicity. In fact they covered his tracks, what there were of them, in case he turned up after a month or so with loss of memory. He was a lonely bird at the best of times, a great walker and naturalist, a curious type to have appealed so strongly to a successful woman. Anyway, the police weren't notified until it was too late for them to do anything, and I was approached after they'd given up. I didn't trouble Miss Wells because that angle had been explored very thoroughly by the authorities and they were quite satisfied that she knew nothing at all about the business."

Dell nodded. He seemed gratified by the final piece of information, which evidently corroborated his own convinced opinion.

"Interesting," he remarked after a pause. "That sort of thing's always happening. I mean one often hears a story like that."

Val looked up in surprise.

"About people walking out into the blue?"

"Yes," he said and smiled at her again. "I've heard of quite half-a-dozen cases in my time. It's quite understandable, of course, but every time it crops up it gives one a jolt, a new vision, like putting on a pair of long-sighted spectacles."

Val was visibly puzzled. She looked very sane sitting up and watching him with something like concern in her eyes.

"How do you mean? What happened to him?"

Dell laughed. He was embarrassed and glanced at Campion for support.

"Well," he said, the colour in his face making his eyes more vivid, "we all do get the feeling that we'd like to walk out, don't we? I mean we all feel at times an insane impulse to vanish, to abandon the great rattling caravan we're driving and walk off down the road with nothing but our own weight to carry. It's not always a question of concrete responsibilities; it's ambitions and conventions and especially affections which seem to get too much at moments. One often feels one'd like to ditch them all and just walk away. The odd thing is that so few of us do, and so when one hears of someone actually succumbing to that most familiar impulse one gets a sort of personal jolt. Portland-Smith is probably selling vacuum cleaners in Philadelphia by now."

Val shook her head.

"Women don't feel like that," she said. "Not alone."

Mr. Campion felt there might be something in this observation but he was not concerning himself with the abstract just then.

Months of careful investigation had led him late the previous afternoon to a little estate in Kent where the young Portland-Smith had spent a summer holiday at the age of nine. During the past ten years the old house had been deserted and had fallen into disrepair, creepers and brambles making of the garden a Sleeping Beauty thicket. There in a natural den in the midst of a shrubbery, the sort of hide-out that any nine-year-old would cherish forever as his own private place, Mr. Campion had found the thirty-eight-year old Portland-Smith, or all that was left of him after three years. The skeleton had been lying face downward, the left arm pillowing the head and the knees drawn up in a feather bed of dried leaves.

(HAPTER 2

$\mathbf{V}$AL'S OFFICE WAS ONE of the more original features of Papendeik's new establishment in Park Lane. Reynarde, who had been responsible for the transformation of the mansion, had indulged in one of his celebrated "strokes of genius" in its construction and Colin Greenleaf's photographs of the white wrought-iron basket of a studio slung under the centre cupola above the well of the grand staircase had appeared in all the more expensive illustrated periodicals at the time of the move.

In spite of its affected design the room was proving unexpectedly useful, much to everyone's relief, for its glass walls afforded a view not only of the visitors' part of the building but a clear vision down the two main workshop corridors and permitted Lady Papendeik to keep an eye on her house.

Although it was technically Val's own domain and contained

a drawing table, Marthe Papendeik sat there most of the day "in the midst of her web," as Rex had once said in a fit of petulance, "looking like a spider, seeing itself a queen bee."

When Marthe Lafranc had come to London in the days when Victorian exuberance was bursting through its confining laces and drawing its breath for the skyrocketing and subsequent crash which were to follow, she had been an acute French businesswoman, hard and brittle as glass and volatile as ether. Her evolution had been accomplished by Papendeik, the great artist. He had taken her as if she had been a bale of tinsel cloth and had created from her something quite unique and individual to himself. "He taught me how to mellow," she said once with a tenderness which was certainly not Gallic, "the *grand seigneur.*"

At sixty she was a small, dark, ugly woman with black silk hair, a lifted face and the gift of making a grace of every fold she wore. She was at her little writing table making great illegible characters with a ridiculous pen when Mr. Campion wandered in after lunch and she greeted him with genuine welcome in her narrow eyes.

"The little Albert," she said. "My dear, the ensemble! Very distinguished. Turn round. Delightful. That is the part of a man one remembers always with affection, his back from the shoulders to the waist. Is Val still on the roof with that mechanic?"

Mr. Campion seated himself and beamed. They were old friends and without the least disrespect he always thought she looked like a little wet newt, she was so sleek and lizardlike with her sharp eyes and swift movements.

"I rather liked him," he said, "but I felt a little superfluous so I came down."

Tante Marthe's bright eyes rested for a moment on two mannequins who were talking together some distance down the southern corridor. The glass walls of the room were sound-proof so there was no means of telling if they were actually saying the things to each other which appearances would suggest, but when one of them caught sight of the little figure silhouetted against the brightness of the further wall there was a hurried adjournment.

Lady Papendeik shrugged her shoulders and made a note of two names on her blotting pad.

"Val is in love with that man," she remarked. "He is very masculine. I hope it is not merely a most natural reaction. We are too many women here. There is no 'body' in the place."

Mr. Campion shied away from the subject.

"You don't like women, Tante Marthe?"

"My dear, it is not a question of liking." The vehemence in her deep, ugly voice startled him. "One does not dislike the half of everything. You bore me, you young people, when you talk about one sex or the other, as if they were separate things. There is only one human entity and that is a man and a woman. The man is the silhouette, the woman is the detail. The one often spoils or makes the other. But apart they are so much material. Don't be a fool."

She turned over the sheet of paper on which she had been writing and drew a little house on it.

"*Did* you like him?" she demanded suddenly, shooting a direct and surprisingly youthful glance at him.

"Yes," he said seriously, "yes. He's a personality and a curiously simple chap, but I liked him."

"The family would raise no difficulty?"

"Val's family?"

"Naturally."

He began to laugh.

"Darling, you're slipping back through the ages, aren't you?"

Lady Papendeik smiled at herself.

"It's marriage, my dear," she confided. "Where marriage is concerned, Albert, I am still French. It is so much better in France. There marriage is always the contract and nobody forgets that, even in the beginning. It makes it so proper. Here no one thinks of his signature until he wants to cross it out."

Mr. Campion stirred uneasily.

"I don't want to be offensive," he murmured, "but I think all this is a bit premature."

"Ah." To his relief she followed him instantly. "I wondered. Perhaps so. Very likely. We will forget it. Why are you here?"

"Come about a body." His tone was diffident. "Nothing indelicate or bad for business, naturally. I want to meet Georgia Wells."

Tante Marthe sat up.

"Georgia Wells," she said. "Of course! I could not think if Portland-Smith was the name of the man or not. Have you the evening paper?"

"Oh, Lord, have they got it already?" He took up the early racing edition from the desk and turned it over. In the Stop Press he found a little paragraph in blurred, irregular type.

SKELETON IN BUSHES.
Papers found near a skeleton
of a man discovered in the
shrubbery of a house near
Wellferry, Kent, suggest that
body may be that of Mr.
Richard Portland-Smith, who

disappeared from his home
nearly three years ago.

He refolded the paper and smiled at her wryly.

"Yes, well, that's a pity," he said.

Lady Papendeik was curious but years of solid experience had taught her discretion.

"It is a professional affair for you?"

"I found the poor chap."

"Ah." She sat nibbling her pen, her small back straight and her inquisitive eyes fixed upon his face. "It is undoubtedly the body of the fiancé?"

"Oh yes, it's Portland-Smith all right. Tante Marthe, was that engagement on or off when he vanished? Do you remember?"

"On," said the old lady firmly. "Ramillies had appeared upon the scene, you understand, but Georgia was still engaged. How long after he disappeared did the wretched man die? Can you tell that?"

"Not from the state of the body...at least I shouldn't think so. It must have been fairly soon but I don't think any pathologist could swear to it within a month or so. However, I fancy the police will be able to pin it down because of the fragments of the clothes. He seems to have been in evening dress."

Tante Marthe nodded. She looked her full age and her lips moved in a little soundless murmur of pity. "And the cause? That will be difficult too?"

"No. He was shot."

She moved her hands and clicked her tongue.

"Very unpleasant," she pronounced and added maliciously:

"It will be interesting to see Ferdie Paul turn it into good publicity."

Campion rose and stood looking down at her, his long thin figure drooping a little.

"I'd better fade away," he said regretfully. "I can't very well butt in on her now."

Lady Papendeik stretched out a restraining hand.

"No, don't go," she said. "You stay. Be intelligent of course; the woman's a client. But I'd like someone to see them all. We are putting up some of the money for Caesar's Court. I would like your advice. Paul and Ramillies will be here and so will Laminoff."

"Caesar's Court?" Campion was surprised. "You too? Everyone I meet seems to have a finger in that pie. You're sitting pretty. It's going to be at Tom Tiddler's ground."

"I think so." She smiled complacently. "London has never had that kind of luxury on the doorstep and we can afford it. It was never possible in the old days because of the transport difficulty and when the transport did come there wasn't the money. Now the two have arrived together. Have you been out there yet? It's hardly a journey at all by car."

"No," said Mr. Campion, grinning. "I don't want to picnic in Naples, take a foam bath, improve my game, eat a lotus or mix with the elite. Also, frankly, the idea of spending six or seven hundred on a week-end party makes me feel physically sick. However, I realise that there are people who do, and I must say I like the wholesale magnificence of the scheme. These things usually flop because the promoters will rely on one or two good features to carry the others. This show *is* solid leather all through. The chef from the Virginia, Teddy Quoit's band, Andy Bullard in charge of the golf course, the Crannis woman doing the swimming and Waugh the tennis, while it was genius to make the place the headquarters of the beauty king chap, what's-his-name."

"Mirabeau," she supplied. "He's an artist. Ditte, his coiffeuse, designed my hair. Yes, the idea was excellent, but the execution has been extraordinary. That's Laminoff. Laminoff was the maître d'hôtel at the Poire d'Or. Bjornson let him in when he crashed. He's incredible, and Madame is no fool. It was Laminoff who insisted that the flying field must be made a customs port. Alan Dell arranged that."

"Dell? Is he in it too?"

"Naturally. All the club planes are Alandel machines and his pilots are in charge. His works are only a mile or so away on the other side of the river. He has a big interest in the whole hotel. That's how Val met him."

"I see." Mr. Campion blinked. "It's quite a neat little miracle of organisation, isn't it? Who's the clever lad in the background? Who woke up in the night with the great idea?"

Tante Marthe hesitated.

"Ferdie Paul. Don't mention it. It's not generally known." She pursed her lips and looked down her long nose. "Do you know Paul?"

"No. I thought he was a stage man. He's a producer, surely?"

"He's very clever," said Lady Papendeik. "He made Georgia Wells and he holds the leases of the Sovereign and the Venture theatres. The Cherry Orchard Club is his and he has a half share in the Tulip Restaurant."

Campion laughed. "And that's all you've been able to find out about him?"

She grimaced at him. "It's not enough, is it?" she said.

"After all, we're not made of money—who is? Oh, they're here, are they? We'll go down."

She nodded and dismissed a page boy who had barely entered the room and had not had time to open his mouth.

"Now," she said without the slightest trace of conscious affectation, "we will see what beautiful dresses can do to a woman. One of these gowns is so lovely that I burst into tears when I first saw it and Rex would have fainted if he hadn't controlled himself, the poor neurotic."

Finding himself incapable of suitable comment, Mr. Campion said nothing and followed her dutifully down the grand staircase.

CHAPTER 3

IT WAS NEVER MR. CAMPION'S custom to make an entrance. In early youth he had perfected the difficult art of getting into and out of rooms without fuss, avoiding both the defensive flourish and the despicable creep, but he swept into Papendeik's grand salon like the rear guard of a conqueror, which in a way, of course, he was.

Lady Papendeik at work was a very different person from Tante Marthe in Val's office. She appeared to be a good two inches higher, for one thing, and she achieved a curious sailing motion which was as far removed from ordinary walking as is the goose step in an exactly opposite direction. Mr. Campion found himself stalking behind her as though to fast and martial music. It was quite an experience.

The salon was golden. Val held that a true conceit is only a vulgarity in the right place and had done the thing thoroughly.

The room itself had been conceived in the grand manner. It was very long and high, with seven great windows leading out on to a stone terrace with bronzes, so that the general effect might easily have become period had not the very pale gold monotone of the walls, floor and furnishings given it a certain conscious peculiarity which, although satisfactory to the eye, was yet not sufficiently familiar to breed any hint of ignorant contempt.

The practical side of the colour scheme, which had really determined the two ladies to adopt it and which was now quite honestly forgotten by both of them, was that as a background for fine silk or wool material there is nothing so flattering as a warm, polished metal. Also, as Tante Marthe had remarked; in an unguarded moment, "gold is so *comforting* my dears, if you can really make it unimportant."

Mr. Campion tramped through pale golden pile and was confronted at last by a vivid group of very human people, all silhouetted, framed and set and thus brought into startling relief against a pale golden wall. He was aware, first of a dark face and then a fair one, a small boy of all unexpected things and afterwards, principally and completely, of Georgia Wells.

She was bigger than he had thought from the auditorium and now, without losing charm, more coarse. She was made up under the skin, as it were, designed by nature as a poster rather than a pen drawing.

He was aware that her eyes were large and grey, with long strong lashes and thick pale skin round them. Even the brown flecks in the grey irises seemed bolder and larger than is common and her expression was bright and shrewd and so frank that he felt she must have known him for some time.

She kissed Lady Papendeik ritualistically upon both cheeks but the gesture was performed absently and he felt that her attention was never diverted an instant from himself.

"Mr. Campion?" she echoed. "Really? Albert Campion?

Her voice, which, like everything else about her, was far stronger and more flexible than the average, conveyed a certain wondering interest and he understood at once that she knew who he was, that she had seen the newspapers and was now considering if there was some fortunate coincidence in their meeting or if it were not fortunate or not a coincidence.

"Ferdie, this is Mr. Campion. *You* know. Mr. Campion, this is Ferdie Paul."

The dark face resolved itself into a person. Ferdie Paul was younger than Mr. Campion had expected. He was a large, plumpish man who looked like Byron. He had the same dark curling hair that was unreasonably inadequate on crown and temples, the same proud, curling mouth which would have been charming on a girl and was not on Mr. Paul, and the same short, strong, uniform features which made him just a little ridiculous, like a pretty bull.

When he spoke, however, the indolence which should have been a part and parcel of his make-up was surprisingly absent. He was a vigorous personality, his voice high and almost squeaky, with a nervous energy in it which never descended into irritability.

There was also something else about him which Campion noticed and could not define. It was a peculiar uncertainty of power, like pinking in a car engine, a quality of labour under difficulties which was odd and more in keeping with his voice than his appearance or personality.

He glanced at Campion with quick, intelligent interest, decided he did not know or need him, and dismissed him from his mind in a perfectly friendly fashion.

"We can begin at once, can't we?" he said to Lady Papendeik. "It's absolutely imperative that they should be quite right."

"They are exquisite," announced Tante Marthe coldly, conveying her irrevocable attitude in one single stroke.

Paul grinned at her. His amusement changed his entire appearance. His mouth became more masculine and the fleeting glimpse of gold stopping in his side teeth made him look for some reason more human and fallible.

"You're a dear, aren't you?" he said and sounded as if he meant it.

Lady Papendeik's narrow eyes, which seemed to be all pupil, flickered at him. She did not smile but her thin mouth quirked and it occurred to Campion, who was watching them, that they were the working brains of the gathering. Neither of them were artists but they were the masters of artists, the Prosperos of their respective Ariels, and they had a very healthy admiration for one another.

By this time new visitors had arrived and were drifting towards the quilted settees between the windows. Rex was very much in evidence. He had lost his anger but retained his pathos, interrupting it at times with little coy exuberances always subdued to the right degree of ingratiating affability.

Campion noticed one woman in particular, a very correctly dressed little matron whose excellent sartorial taste could not quite lend her elegance, finding him very comforting. He wondered who she was and why she should receive such deference. Rex, he felt certain, would genuinely only find charm where it was politic that charm should be found, yet she did not by her manner appear to be very rich nor did she seem to belong to anybody. He had little time to observe her or anyone else, however, for Georgia returned to him.

"I'm so interested in you," she said with a frankness which he found a little overwhelming. "I'm not at all sure you couldn't be useful to me."

The naïveté of the final remark was so complete that for a second he wondered if she had really made it, but her eyes, which were as grey as tweed suiting and rather like it, were fixed on his own and her broad, beautiful face was earnest and friendly.

"Something rather awful has happened to me this afternoon," she went on, her voice husky. "They've found the skeleton of a man I adored. I can't help talking about it to somebody. Do forgive me. It's the shock, you know."

She gave him a faint apologetic smile and it came to him with surprise that she was perfectly sincere. He learnt a great deal about Georgia Wells at that moment and was interested in her. The ordinary hysteric who dramatises everything until she loses all sense of proportion and becomes a menace to the unsuspecting stranger was familiar to him, but this was something new. For the moment at any rate Georgia Wells was genuine in her despair and she seemed to be regarding him not as an audience but as a possible ally, which was at least disarming.

"I ought not to blurt it out like this to a stranger," she said. "I only realise how terrible these things are when I hear myself saying them. It's disgusting. Do forgive me."

She paused and looked up into his face with sudden child-like honesty.

"It is a frightful shock, you know."

"Of course it is," Campion heard himself saying earnestly. "Terrible. Didn't you know he was dead?"

"No. I had no idea." The protest was hearty and convincing but it lacked the confiding quality of her earlier announcements and he glanced at her sharply. She closed her eyes and opened them again.

"I'm behaving damnably," she said. "It's because I've heard so much about you I feel I know you. This news about Richard has taken me off my balance. Come and meet my husband."

He followed her obediently and it occurred to him as they crossed the room that she had that rare gift, so rare that he had some difficulty in remembering that it was only a gift, of being able to talk directly to the essential individual lurking behind the civilised facade of the man before her, so that it was impossible for him to evade or disappoint her without feeling personally responsible.

"Here he is," said Georgia. "Mr. Campion, this is my husband."

Campion's involuntary thought on first meeting Sir Raymond Ramillies was that he would be a particularly nasty drunk. This thought came out of the air and was not inspired by anything faintly suggestive of the alcoholic in the man himself. From Ramillies' actual appearance there was nothing to indicate that he ever drank at all, yet when Campion was first confronted by that arrogant brown face with the light eyes set too close together and that general air of irresponsible power the first thing that came into his mind was that it was as well that the fellow was at least sober.

They shook hands and Ramillies stood looking at him in a way that could only be called impudent. He did not speak at all but seemed amused and superior without troubling to be even faintly antagonistic.

Mr. Campion continued to regard him with misgiving and all the odd stories he had heard about this youthful middle-aged man with the fine-sounding name returned to his mind. Ramillies had retired from a famous regiment after the Irish trouble, at which times fantastic and rather horrible rumours had been floating about in connection with his name. There had been a brief period of sporting life in the shires and then he had been given the governorship of Ulangi, an unhealthy spot on the West Coast, a tiny serpent of country separating two foreign possessions. There the climate was so inclement that he was forced to spend three months of the year at home, but it was hinted that he contrived to make his exile not unexciting. Campion particularly remembered a pallid youngster who had been one of a party to spend a month at the Ulangi Residency and who had been strangely loth to discuss his adventures there on his return. One remark had stuck in Campion's mind: "Ramillies is a funny bird. All the time you're with him you feel he's going to get himself hanged or win the V.C. then and there before your eyes. Wonderful lad. Puts the wind up you."

Ramillies was quiet enough at the moment. He had made no remark of any kind since their arrival, but had remained standing with his feet apart and his hands behind him. He was swinging a little on his toes and his alert face wore an expression of innocence which was blatantly deceptive. Campion received the uncomfortable impression that he was thinking of something to do.

"I've just blurted out all my misery about Richard." Georgia's deep voice was devoid of any affectation and indeed achieved a note of rather startling sincerity. "I had no idea how frightfully shaken up I am. You know who Mr. Campion is, don't you, Raymond?"

"Yes, of course I do." Ramillies glanced at his wife as he spoke and his thin sharp voice, which had yet nothing effeminate about it, was amused. He looked at Campion and spoke to him as though from a slight distance. "Do you find that sort of thing terribly interesting? I suppose you do or you wouldn't do it. There's a thrill in it, is there, hunting down fellows?"

The interesting thing was that he was not rude. His voice, manner and even the words were all sufficiently offensive to warrant one knocking him down, but the general effect was somehow naïve. There was no antagonism there at all, rather something wistful in the final question.

Mr. Campion suddenly remembered him at school, a much older boy who had gone on to Sandhurst at the end of Campion's first term, leaving a banner of legend behind him. With a touch of snobbism which he recognised as childish at the time he refrained from mentioning the fact.

"The thrill is terrific," he agreed solemnly. "I frequently frighten myself into a fit with it."

"Do you?" Again there was the faint trace of real interest.

Georgia put her arm through Campion's, an unself-conscious gesture designed to attract his attention, which it did.

"Why did you come to see this dress show?"

He felt her shaking a little as she clung to him.

"I wanted to meet you," he said truthfully. "I wanted to talk to you."

"About Richard? I'll tell you anything I know. I want to talk about him."

While there was no doubt about her sincerity there was

a suggestion of daring in her manner, an awareness of danger without the comprehension of it, which gave him his first real insight into her essential character and incidentally half startled the life out of him.

"You said he was dead, Raymond." There was a definite challenge in her voice and Campion felt her quivering like a discharging battery at his side.

"Oh yes, I knew the chap was dead." Ramillies was remarkably matter of fact and Campion stared at him.

"How did you know?"

"Thought he must be, else he'd have turned up once I'd gone back to Africa and Georgia was alone." He made the statement casually but with conviction and it dawned upon the other man that he was not only indifferent to any construction that might be put upon his words, but incapable of seeing that they might convey any other meaning.

Georgia shuddered. Campion felt the involuntary movement and was puzzled again, since it did not seem to be inspired purely by fear or disgust. He had the unreasonable impression that there was something more like pleasure at the root of it.

"If it wouldn't upset you to talk about him," he ventured, looking down at her, "I'd like to hear your impression of his mental condition the last time you saw him…if you're sure you don't mind."

"My dear, I *must* talk!" Georgia's cry came from the heart, or seemed to do so, but the next instant her grip on his arm loosened and she said in an entirely different tone: "Who's that coming over here with Val?"

Campion glanced up and was aware of a faint sense of calamity.

"That?" he murmured guiltily. "Oh, that's Alan Dell, the aeroplane chap."

"Introduce us," said Georgia. "I think he wants to meet me."

Val came across the room purposefully and it occurred to Mr. Campion that she looked like the *Revenge* sailing resolutely into battle with her pennants flying. She looked very fine with her little yellow coxcomb held high and every line of her body flowing with that particular kind of femininity which is neat and precisely graceful. He sighed for her. He was prepared to back the Spanish galleon every time.

Alan Dell came beside her. Having once met the man, Campion discovered that his shy and peculiarly masculine personality was now completely apparent and that his first superficial impression of him had vanished.

Georgia put about.

"My pretty," she said, stretching out both hands. "Come and comfort me with clothes. I'm in a tragedy."

Her fine strong body was beautiful as she swung forward and a warmth of friendliness went out to meet the other girl. Val responded to it cautiously.

"I've got just the dress for it, whatever it is," she said lightly. "The ultimate garment of all time."

Georgia drew back. She looked pathetically hurt behind her smile.

"I'm afraid it's a real tragedy," she said reproachfully.

"My pet, I'm so sorry. What is it?" Val made the apology so unjustly forced from her and her eyes grew wary.

Georgia glanced over her shoulder before she spoke. Ramillies still stood swinging on his toes, his glance resting consideringly upon the small boy in the corner. Georgia shook her head.

"Tell me about the lovely dresses," she said, and added before Val or Campion could speak, "Who is this?" a demand which brought Dell forward with the conviction that there had been a general disinclination to present him.

He shook hands with unexpected gaucherie and stood blinking at her, suffering no doubt from that misapprehension so common to shy folk, that he was not quite so clearly visible to her as she was to him.

Georgia regarded him with that glowing and intelligent interest which was her chief weapon of attack.

"The second last person on earth to find in a dress shop," she said. "My dear, are you going to enjoy all this? Have you ever been to this sort of show before?"

"No," he said and laughed. "I stayed to see you."

Georgia blushed. The colour flowed up her throat and over her face, with a charm no seventeen-year-old could have touched.

"That's very nice of you," she said. "I'm afraid I'm going to be very dull. Something rather beastly has happened to me and I'm just behaving disgustingly and blurting it out to everyone."

It was a dangerous opening and might well have proved disastrous but that her gift of utter directness was a lodestone. Dell's sudden gratified sense of kindly superiority was communicated to them all and he murmured something bald about seeing her in trouble once more.

"*The Little Sacrifice?*" she said quickly. "Oh, I adored that woman Jacynth. I found myself putting all I'd ever known or ever felt into her, poor sweetie. It was very nice of you to go and see me."

From that moment her manner changed subtly. It was such a gradual metamorphosis, so exquisitely done, that. Campion only just noticed it, but the fact remained that she began to remind him strongly of the heroine in *The Little Sacrifice*. Touches of the character crept into her voice, into helpless little gestures, into her very attitude of mind, and he thought ungenerously that it would have been even more interesting, besides being much more easy to follow, if the original part had only been played in some strong foreign accent.

Dell was openly enchanted. He remained watching her with fascinated attention, his blue eyes smiling and very kind.

"It was a long time ago and all very sad and silly even then." Georgia sounded both brave and helplessly apologetic. "He was such a dear, my sweet moody Richard. I knew him so awfully well. We were both innately lonely people and…well, we were very fond of one another. When he simply vanished I was broken-hearted, but naturally I couldn't admit it. Could I?"

She made a little fluttering appeal to them all to understand.

"One doesn't, does one?" she demanded with that sudden frankness which, if it is as embarrassing, is also as entirely disarming as nakedness. "I mean, when one really is in love one's so painfully self-conscious, so miserably mistrustful of one's own strength. I'm, talking about the real, rather tragic thing, of course. Then one's so horribly afraid that this exquisite, precious, deliriously lovely sanctuary one's somehow achieved may not be really solid, may not be one's own for keeps. One's so conscious all the time that one can be hurt beyond the bounds of bearing that in one's natural pessimism one dreads disaster all the time, and so when something does happen one accepts it and crawls away somewhere. You do know what I mean, don't you?"

They did, of course, being all adult and reasonably experienced, and Mr. Campion, who was shocked, was yet grudgingly impressed. Her tremendous physical health and that quality which Dell had called "confiding" had clothed an embarrassing revelation of the ordinary with something rather charming. He glanced at Val.

She looked past him and did not speak aloud, although her lips moved. He thought he read the words "strip tease," and regarded her with sudden respect.

Georgia did not let the scene drop.

"I'm so sorry," she said helplessly. "This is all so disgustingly vulgar of me, but oh, my dears!—suddenly to see it on the placards, to make Ferdie leap out of the car and get a paper, to snatch it away from him and then to look and find it all true! They've found his skeleton, you see."

Her eyes were holding them all and there was real wretchedness in the grey shadows.

"You never think of people you know having skeletons, do you?"

"My dear, how horrible!" Val's ejaculation was startled out of her. "When did all this happen?"

"Now," said Georgia miserably. "Now, just as I was coming here. I'd have gone home, my pet, but I couldn't let you and everybody else down just when we were all so rushed. I didn't realise it was going to have this dreadful loquacious effect upon me."

"Darling, what are you talking about?" Ferdie Paul slipped his arm round her and drew her back against him. His face over her shoulder was dark and amused, but there was more in his voice than tolerance. "Forget it. You'll upset yourself."

Georgia shivered, smiled and released herself with a gentle dignity, directed, Campion felt, at himself and Dell. She glanced at her husband, who came forward promptly, his natural springy walk lending him a jauntiness which added considerably to his disturbing air of active irresponsibility.

"That's right, Georgia," he said in his flat staccato voice. "Forget the fellow if you can, and if you can't don't make an ass of yourself."

Even he seemed to feel that this admonition might sound a trifle harsh to the uninitiated, for he suddenly smiled with that transfiguring, sunny happiness usually associated with early childhood. "What I mean to say is, a lovely girl looks very touching grizzling over a corpse but she looks damned silly doing it over a skeleton. She's missed the boat. The great lover's not merely dead, dearest; he's dead and gone. Should I be a bounder if I asked for a drink?"

The last remark was directed towards Val with a quick-eyed charm which was ingratiating.

"Certainly not. You must all need one." Val sounded thoroughly startled. She glanced at Rex, who had been hovering on the edge of the group, and he nodded and disappeared. Ferdie Paul resumed his hold on Georgia. He had a gently contemptuous way with her, as if she were a difficult elderly relative of whom he was fond.

"We're going to see the great dress for the third act first," he said. "I want to make sure that when Pendleton gets you by the throat he can only tear the left shoulder out. It's got to be restrained and dignified. I don't want you running about in your brassière. The whole danger of that scene is that it may go a bit *vieux jeu* if we don't look out...nineteen twenty-sixish or so. Lady Papendeik wants us to see the dress on the model first because apparently it's pretty hot. Then I want you to get into it and we'll run through that bit."

Georgia stiffened.

"I'm not going to rehearse here in front of a lot of strangers," she protested. "God knows I'm not temperamental, sweetheart, but there are limits. You're not going to ask me to do that, Ferdie, not this afternoon of all times?"

"Georgia." Paul's arm had tightened, and Campion saw hiss round brown eyes fixed firmly upon the woman's own with a terrifying quality of intelligence in them, as if he were trying to hypnotise some sense into her. "Georgia, you're not going to be silly, are you, *dear?*"

It was an idiotic little scene, reminding Campion irresistibly of a jockey he had once heard talking to a refractory horse.

"We'll go. Mr. Campion and I will go, Miss Wells." Alan Dell spoke hastily and Paul, looking up, seemed to see him for the first time.

"Oh no, that's all right," he said: "There's only a few of us here. It's a purely technical matter. You're going to be reasonable, aren't you, darling? You're only a bit jittery because of the boy friend."

Georgia smiled at him with unexpected tolerance and turned to Dell with a little deprecating grimace.

"My nerves have gone to pieces," she said and it occurred to Mr. Campion that she might easily be more accurate than she realised.

It was at this moment that Tante Marthe came over with one of her small coloured pages at her elbow.

"The *Trumpet* is on the phone, my dear," she said. "Will you speak to them?"

Georgia's hunted expression would have been entirely convincing if it had not been so much what one might have expected.

"All right," she said heavily. "This is the horrible part of it all. This is what I've been dreading. Yes, I'll come."

"No." Ramillies and Paul spoke together and paused to look at one another afterwards. It was the briefest interchange of glances and Mr. Campion, who was watching them both, became aware for the first time that the undercurrent which he had been trying to define throughout the entire afternoon was an unusual, and in the circumstances incomprehensible, combination of alarm and excitement.

"No," said Ramillies again. "Don't say a thing."

"Do you mean that?" She turned to him almost with eagerness and he did not look at her.

"No, dear, I don't think I would." Ferdie Paul spoke casually. "We'll put out some sort of statement later if it's necessary. It's not a particularly good story so they won't get excited. Tell them Miss Wells is not here. She left half an hour ago."

The page went off obediently and Paul watched the child until it disappeared, his figure drooping and his prominent eyes thoughtful. Georgia looked at Dell, who moved over to her.

"That must be a very great relief to you," he said.

She stared at him. "You understand, don't you?" she said with sudden earnestness. "You really do."

Mr. Campion turned away rather sadly and became aware of Val. She was looking at the other woman and he caught her unawares. Once again she surprised him. Jealousy is one emotion but hatred is quite another and much more rare in a civilised community. Once it is seen it is not easily forgotten.

CHAPTER 4

THE GENTLE ART OF putting things over had always interested Mr. Campion, but as he sat down beside Alan Dell to watch the house of Papendeik at work he was aware of a sudden sense of irritation. There was so much going on under his nose that needed explanation. The strangers were vivid personalities but not types he recognised and at the moment he did not understand their reactions at all.

Meanwhile an impressive if informal performance was beginning. Val and Tante Marthe were staging an act and he was entertained to note that they worked together with the precision of a first-class vaudeville turn.

Tante Marthe had seated herself on the largest of the settees between the two most central windows and had made room for Ferdie Paul beside her, while Georgia had been provided by Rex with a wide-seated gilt chair thrust out into the room a little.

She sat in it regally, her dark head thrown back and her lovely broad face tilted expectantly. Even so she contrived to look a little tragic, making it clear that she was a woman with a background of deep emotional experience.

Val stood behind her, slender and exquisite and very much the brilliant young artist about to display something that might well prove to be the masterpiece of a century.

The rest of the conversation piece was furnished by the staff. Every available saleswoman had assembled together at one end of the room, as though for prayers in an old-fashioned household. There was a flutter of expectancy among them, a gathering together to admire a creation for which they all took a small degree of personal responsibility. Their very presence indicated a big moment.

Dell caught Campion's eye and leant forward.

"Wonderfully interesting," he whispered with professional appreciation.

There was a moment of silence and Rex slid forward to give an entirely unnecessary flick to the folds of a curtain. Lady Papendeik glanced round her and raised a small dark paw. The staff sighed and the dress appeared.

At this point Mr. Campion felt somewhat out of his depth.

He looked at the dress and saw that it was long and white, with a satisfactory arrangement of drapery at the front, and that it had an extraordinary-looking girl in it. She caught his attention because she was beautiful without being in any way real or desirable. She had a strong superficial likeness to Georgia inasmuch as she was not small and was dark with broad cheekbones, but there all similarity ended. Where Georgia was coarse the newcomer was exquisite, where Georgia was vital the other girl was dead.

Campion glanced at Tante Marthe and was delighted to see her sitting back, her hands in her lap, her eyes half closed and an outrageous expression of fainting ecstasy on her face. Ferdie Paul looked thoughtful but by no means unimpressed and the staff whispered and preened itself.

Campion and Alan Dell looked at the gown again, each trying to discover why it should be so particularly pleasing, and were both on the verge of making the same thundering mistake by deciding that its charm lay in its simplicity when Georgia dropped the bomb.

"Val, my angel," she said, her lovely husky voice sounding clearly through the room, "it's breath-taking! It's *you*. It's *me*. But, my pet, it's not *new*. I saw it last night at the Dudley Club."

There was a moment of scandalised silence. The Greek chorus in the corner gaped and Rex's nervous giggle echoed inopportunely from the background. The formal conversation piece had turned into a Gluyas Williams picture.

Lady Papendeik rose.

"My dear," she said, "my dear." Her voice was not very loud or even particularly severe but instantly all the humour went out of the situation and Georgia was on the defensive.

"Oh, my dear, I'm so sorry." She turned to Val impulsively and the most ungenerous among them could not have doubted her honesty. "There's been some hideous mistake, of course. This whole day is like a nightmare. I did see it. I saw it last night and it fascinated me. I can even prove it, unfortunately. There's a photograph of the Blaxill woman wearing it in one of the morning papers...the *Range Finder*, I think...on the back page. She's dancing with a cabinet minister. I noticed it, naturally. It wiped the floor with everything else."

Val said nothing. Her face was quite expressionless as she nodded to the horrified group at the other end of the room. There was a discreet scurrying towards the door and a rustle of chatter as they reached the hall. Georgia stood up. Her tall, graceful body towered over Val, making the other girl look as if she belonged to some smaller and neater world.

"Of course it hadn't your cut," she said earnestly, "and I don't think it was in that material, but it was white."

Lady Papendeik shrugged her shoulders.

"That is Bouleau's *Caresse*," she said, "woven to our design."

Georgia looked like helpless apology personified.

"I had to tell you," she said.

"Of course you did, my dear," murmured Lady Papendeik without thawing. "Of course."

There was no doubt that the incident was a major catastrophe. Everybody began to talk and Paul crossed the room to Val's side, with Ramillies, casual and unaccountable, at his heels.

Mr. Campion was puzzled. In his experience the duplication of a design, although the most dispiriting of all disasters to the artist concerned, is seldom taken seriously by anyone else, unless hard money has already been involved, and he began to wonder if this explosion was not in the nature of a safety valve, seized upon gratefully because it was a legitimate excuse for excitement actually engendered by something less politic to talk about.

The other person who might possibly have shared Mr. Campion's own Alice in Wonderland view of the situation was the small boy. He sat staring into the inside of his Haverleigh cap, his forehead wrinkled, and was apparently unaware of any crisis.

The return of Rex was dramatic. He came hurrying in with a perfectly white face, a newspaper in his outstretched hand. Lady Papendeik stood looking at the photograph for some moments and when she spoke her comment was typical.

"Only a thief would permit a woman with a stomach to commit such sacrilege. Who dresses her?"

The others crowded round and Dell turned to Campion again.

"It's a leakage," he murmured. "You can't stop it in any show where designs are secret. It's an infuriating thing."

"It's a miracle the photograph is so clear," said Georgia forlornly. "They're usually so vague. But you can't miss that, can you? It was in ribbed silk. I couldn't take my eyes off it." She put an arm round Val's shoulders. "You poor sweet," she said.

Val released herself gently and turned to Rex.

"Who is that woman's couturier?"

"Ring her up." Rsmillies made the outrageously impolitic suggestion with all the vigorous irresponsibility which turned him into such a peculiarly disturbing element. "Say you're a magazine. Georgia, you do it...or I will. Shall I?"

"No, darling, of course not. Don't be an ass." Georgia had spoken casually and he turned to her.

"Ass be damned!" he exploded with a violence which startled everyone. "It's the only intelligent suggestion that's been put forward so far. What's the woman's name? She'll be in the book, I suppose."

His fury was so entirely unexpected that for a moment the main disaster was forgotten. Campion stared at him in astonishment. His thin jaws were clenched and the little pulses in them throbbed visibly. The reaction was so entirely out of proportion to the occurrence that Campion was inclined to suspect that the man was drunk after all, when he caught a glimpse of Ferdie Paul. Both he and Georgia were eyeing Ramillies with definite apprehension.

"Wait a moment, old boy." Paul sounded cautious. "You never know. We may be able to pin it down here.

"You may in an hour or so of fooling about." Ramillies' contempt was bitter. "But that's the straightforward, elementary way of finding a thing out...ask."

"Just one little moment," murmured Tante Marthe over her shoulder. "This is not a thing that has never happened before."

Ramillies shrugged his shoulders. "As you please. But I still think the intelligent thing to do is to get on the phone to the woman. Tell her all about it if you must. But if I was doing it myself I should say I was a magazine and get it out of her that way. However, it's nothing to do with me, thank God."

He swung on his heel and made for the door.

"Ray, where are you going?" Georgia still sounded apprehensive.

He paused on the threshold and regarded her with cold dislike which was uncomfortably convincing.

"I'm simply going downstairs to see if they've got a telephone book," he said and went out.

Val glanced at Georgia, a startled question in her eyes, but it was Ferdie Paul who answered her.

"Oh no, that's all right. He won't phone," he said and looked across at the small boy, who nodded reassuringly and, sliding off his chair, passed unobtrusively out of the room. It was an odd incident and Dell glanced at Campion.

"Astonishing chap," he said under his breath and regarded Georgia with increased interest.

Meanwhile Rex, who had been permitted to get a word

in at last, was talking earnestly to Tante Marthe. He had a nervous habit of wriggling ingratiatingly and now, all the time he was talking, he seemed to be making surreptitious attempts to stroke his calves by leaning over backwards to get at them. But his observations were to the point.

"I know Leonard Lôke used to dress her," he said, "and if the design has gone there, of course it means it'll be turned over to the worst kind of wholesalers and produced by the hundred. It's a tragedy."

"The premier who made it, the vendeuse, Mr. s Saluski, the child in the fitting room, you, myself and Val," murmured Lady Papendeik, shooting her little lizard head up. "No one else saw the finished dress. The sketch was never completed. Val cut it on the living model."

Rex straightened.

"Wait, he said in an altered voice. "I've remembered. Leonard Lôke is two partners, Pretzger and Morris. Pretzger had a brother-in-law in the fur trade. You may remember him, madame; we've dealt with him once or twice. A fortnight ago I saw that man dining at the Borgia in Greek Street and he had Miss Adamson with him."

The dramatic point of this statement was not clear to Mr. Campion at first but, as all eyes were slowly turned upon the one person in the room who had hitherto taken no interest whatever in the proceedings, the inference dawned slowly upon him.

The mannequin had remained exactly where she was when the general attention had first been distracted from her. She was standing in the middle of the room, beautiful, serene and entirely remote. Her lack of reality was almost unpleasant and it occurred to Campion that her personality was as secret as if she had been a corpse. Now, with everyone staring at her rather than her dress, she did not come to life but remained looking at them blankly with brilliant, foolish eyes.

"Caroline, is this true?" demanded Tante Marthe.

"Is what true, madame?" Her voice, a jew's-harp with a Croydon accent, came as a shock to some of them. Campion, who knew from experience that the beauty of porcelain lies too often in the glaze, was not so much surprised as regretfully confirmed in an opinion.

"Don't be a fool, my dear." Lady Papendeik betrayed unexpected heartiness. "You must know if you've eaten with a man or not. Do not let us waste time."

"I didn't know whose brother-in-law he was," protested Miss Adamson sulkily.

"Did you describe the model? Did it slip out by accident? These things have happened."

"No, I didn't tell him, madame."

"You understand what has occurred?"

Miss Adamson did not change her expression. Her dark eyes were liquid and devastatingly unintelligent.

"I didn't tell him anything. I swear it, I didn't."

Tante Marthe sighed. "Very well. Go and take it off."

As the girl floated from the room Val made a gesture of resignation.

"That's all we shall ever know," she said to Dell, who was standing beside her. "There's a direct link there, of course, but she was quite emphatic."

Campion joined them.

"I thought I noticed a certain clinging to the letter," he ventured.

"That was the diagnosis that leapt to my mind but I

didn't care to mention it," Dell said, and added with the smile which made him attractive, "She's too lovely to be that kind of fool."

"No one's too lovely to be mental, in my experience," remarked Lady Papendeik briskly. "What diagnosis is this?"

"We thought she might be a letter-of-the-law liar," Dell said, glancing at Campion for support. "She didn't tell the man, she drew it for him. They're the most impossible people in the world to deal with. If you pin them down they get more and more evasive and convince themselves all the time that they're speaking the literal truth which they are, of course, in a way. In my experience the only thing to do is to get rid of them, however valuable they are. Still, I shouldn't like to convict the girl on that evidence alone."

Tante Marthe hesitated and it went through Campion's mind that she was suppressing a remark that might possibly turn out to be indiscreet.

Ferdie Paul, who had remained silent throughout the interview, looked down at her.

"Send her to Caesar's Court," he said. "She's too lovely to lose. Margaret is down there, isn't she? Turn this kid over to her. She can talk about the gowns there as much as she likes; she won't see them until they're ready to be shown."

"Perhaps so," said Tante Marthe and her black eyes wavered.

Georgia resumed her seat.

"I think you're very generous, Val," she began. "I'm broken-hearted. I could weep. You'll never make me anything so deliriously lovely again."

"No," Val said, a cloud passing over her face, "I don't suppose I ever shall."

Georgia stretched out a strong hand and drew the other girl towards her.

"Darling, that was mean," she said with a sweet gentleness which was out of period, let alone character. "You're upset because your lovely design has been stolen. You're naturally livid and I understand that. But you're lucky, you know. After all, Val, it's such a little thing. I hate to repeat all this but I can't get it off my mind. Richard's poor murdered body has been found and here are we all fooling about stupid idiot dresses for a stupid idiot play."

She did not turn away but sat looking at them and her eyes slowly filled with tears and brimmed over. If she had only sounded insincere, only been not quite so unanswerably in the right, the outburst would have been forgivable: as it was, they all stood round uncomfortably until Mr. Campion elected to drop his little brick.

"I say, you know, you're wrong there," he said in his quiet, slightly nervous voice. "I don't think the word 'murder' has gone through any official mind. Portland-Smith committed suicide; that's absolutely obvious, to the police at any rate."

Val, who knew him, guessed from his expression of affable innocence that he hoped for some interesting reaction to this announcement, but neither of them was prepared for what actually took place, Georgia sat up stiffly in her chair and stared at him, while a dark stream of colour rose up her throat, swelling the veins in her neck and passing over her expressionless face.

"That's not true," she said.

With what appeared to be well-meaningness of the most unenlightened kind, Mr. Campion persisted in his point, ignoring all the danger signals.

"Honestly," he said. "I can reassure you on that question. I'm hand in glove with the fellow who found the body. As a matter of fact I was actually on the spot myself this morning. The poor chap had killed himself all right...At least that's what the coroner will decide; I'm sure of it."

The quiet plausible voice was conversational and convincing.

"No." Georgia made the word a statement. "I don't believe it. It's not true." She was controlling herself with difficulty and when she stood up her body was trembling with the effort. There was no doubt at all about her principal emotion and it was so unaccountable and unreasonable in the circumstances that even Mr. Campion showed some of the astonishment he felt. She was angry, beside herself with ordinary, unadulterated rage.

Campion looked to Ferdie Paul for assistance, but he did not intervene. He stood regarding her speculatively, almost, it seemed to Campion, with the same sort of puzzled conjecture that he felt himself.

It was left to Tante Marthe to make the enquiry that was on the tip of everybody's tongue.

"My dear child," she said with faint reproof, in her tone, "why be so annoyed? The poor man has been dead these three years. Had he been murdered it must have meant that someone killed him and that would entail trouble for everyone who knew him. If he killed himself no one need think of him with anything except pity."

"Oh, don't be so silly, angel." Georgia turned on the old woman in exasperation. "Can't you see the damage a story like that can do once it gets about? I won't believe it. I know it's not true."

"You know?" Campion's eyes were mild behind his spectacles but they did not disarm her into answering him impulsively.

"Richard was not a suicidal type," she said after a pause which lasted too long. "This is the final insufferable straw. I can't bear it. You must all forgive me and manage as best you can. I must go home."

"Going home?" Ramillies' voice sounded disappointed in the doorway. "Why? What's the matter now?" He seemed to have forgotten his flamboyant exit of ten minutes before, and came in jauntily pleased with himself as ever.

Georgia stood looking at him steadily.

"Albert Campion says Richard committed suicide. He seems to think there's no doubt about it."

"Oh?" Ramillies' casualness was remarkable and Campion wished he knew the man better. From what he had seen of him so far the reaction might mean absolutely anything, even genuine disinterest. Since no one else spoke it came to Ramillies somewhat belatedly that further comment was expected. "It's a long time ago anyhow," he remarked with singularly unhappy effect. "There'll be no ferreting about either, which is one good thing. That's the one advantage of suicide; everyone knows who did it," he ended lamely, and remained looking at his wife.

Georgia kept her eyes upon him for almost a minute and, having subdued him, turned to Dell.

"Would you be most terribly kind and drive me home?"

"Why, yes. Yes, of course." He looked a little startled. "Of course," he repeated. "I'd like to."

"Bless you," said Georgia and smiled at him faintly.

"Oh, I'll take you home if you really want to go," put in Ramillies without much enthusiasm.

She drew away from him.

"I'm not sure if I ever want to speak to you again," she said distinctly and went out, taking Dell with her.

"What on earth did she mean by that?" demanded Ferdie Paul.

Ramillies turned to look at him and there was, incongruously, the suggestion of a smile in the many creases round his eyes.

"God knows, my dear fellow," he said. "God knows."